Hushwing
Ghost-Owl

Grey Pelt: Spirit of the Last Wolf

The Second Moon Map Chronicle

D'ARCY
WOLF-SHADOW

More Magical Adventures
of an English Setter Pack

Nina Green

Pendragon
press ltd

D'Arcy Wolf-Shadow

Copyright © 2011 Nina Green

Published in 2011 by
Pendragon Press Ltd.
E-mail: books@pendragon-press-ltd.co.uk
www.pendragon-press-ltd.co.uk

A CIP catalogue record for this book is
available from the British Library.

ISBN 978 0 9530538 4 1

*Printed and bound in Wales by
Dinefwr Press Ltd.
Rawlings Road, Llandybie
Carmarthenshire, SA18 3YD*

Cover illustrations:

Front:
Bottom left: D'Arcy.
Top right: Grey Pelt (Canadian Wolf: © Zastavkin | Dreamstime.com).

Back: Full moon at Winter Solstice (© RegienPassaan | Dreamstime.com).
D'Arcy and Destiny (Ian Mulroy).

Frontispieces: 'Hushwing Ghost-Owl' (photo taken by Kevin Keatley and supplied
by the Barn Owl Trust).
'Grey Pelt: Spirit of the Last Wolf'
('Wolf Spirit' by Jason Yoder | Dreamstime.com).

D'Arcy Wolf-Shadow can be ordered from bookshops,
on-line from Amazon
or direct from the Pendragon Press Ltd website:
www.pendragon-press-ltd.co.uk

This book is dedicated with much love to:
Sh. Ch. Moorbrook Just Joey

'Joey'

16th April, 1999 – 5th July, 2010

Ben's son
And wise Top Dog, dear friend and
much-loved family member.

'Always a Showman, ever a Winner.'

Trot on Joey: pace your lap of honour in the
Great Ring of Stars in the Sky.

TO/JEAN HAPPY BIRTHDAY
HAPPY READING!
LOVE
STEPHEN
X

Contents

Copyright Photographs

Acknowledgements

Heartfelt thanks to Lorna and Ken for our wonderful 'Mr. D'Arcy'. He is profoundly loving and full of character with a dash of audacity when it comes to 'wooing' his beloved Alpha-She! My first boy: very precious, and so much loved by us both. Grateful thanks too for the delightful and mischievous Clifford, who has excelled himself by siring nine beautiful puppies, and giving us the longed-for Baby Benson. Thank you, Lorna, for overcoming that initial resistance and for opening my heart to the incomparable delight of Setter Boys!

Grateful thanks also to the Committee and all the members of the English Setter Association for the admirable support given to the first *Moon Map* book and now to this, the sequel. Special thanks to Mr. Elwyn Evans for his invaluable help and advice, and to Chris Bird for his professional website features of the *Moon Map* books – and to both for their friendly and enjoyable anecdotes and 'Setter Chat!'

I also wish to thank photographer Simon Frazier for permitting me to use the striking study of his Wolf-dog Bleiz loping through the forest. Over time, Simon has worked closely and in deep empathy with the wolves, and is an impressive source of knowledge.

Grateful thanks as always to 'Dr. Ian' at Galemire Veterinary Hospital for his compassionate and exceptional care of our Setter family and sharp sense of humour that always raises a smile. These days, ready access to a good vet is priceless; I have the best.

As always enduring love and gratitude to husband Jim for his deep love of the Setters – and his unfazed acceptance of each new arrival! Also love and thanks to our son Craig for his understanding and sharing of the creative highs and lows, and for acting as 'chauffeur' and companion on my 'Setter trips'.

Setter Love is a truly magical thing; I hope this book does it justice.

"I live in his shadow. At times I feel him within me, mostly as Lady Moon reaches her full power and glory . . . It is then that the urge to lope freely over field and mountain, to poise on a summit, tilt my head and open my throat to give voice is strongest – and hardest to resist."

Hello there: it's me again, Ben . . .

Many of you will know me already from the first Moon Map Chronicle, but for those whom I haven't met before I am an English Setter, late Pack Leader and Sire, and it is my task now to relate the Pack Chronicles from beyond the Rainbow Bridge.

In that first book I introduced the founder members of our pack and ended with the present day ones and the arrival of Flossie and Fenella the Third. They are all here once more to share with you their Pack life and adventures; but one of them will move to centre-stage. I'm sure you will remember the pups' Uncle D'Arcy who is also my much-loved grandson. He is the big, handsome 'blue' lad who resembles his Great Aunt Fenella the Second in both looks and ways: the courage of a lion with the comedy of a clown! However, in his quiet moments he shares her dignity too.

But they also share something deeper. Like Fenella, he too was touched by Grey Pelt and will forever carry his mark. He is now six years old and maturing fast. So let us see what he will make of his ghostly legacy . . .

Merlins Mere

1.

Disquiet . . .

I live in his shadow. At times I feel him within me, mostly as Lady Moon reaches her full power and glory and lights the heavens. I feel it even when clouds billow and veil her face. The pull is unmistakeable and the power tingles along my nerves causing my muscles to twitch. It is then that the urge to lope freely over field and mountain, to poise on a summit, tilt my head and open my throat to give voice is strongest – and hardest to resist.

This then was the essence of D'Arcy's deep and dark thoughts as he gazed at his image reflected on the surface of Merlins Mere, named for the falcons that roost in the stand of rowan trees at the far end. He carries the same burden as his great aunt Fenella. She also had the sable face mask that he saw now darkening his reflection, but in him this sign is pronounced by the black line that streaks from left eye to ear, so that Alpha-She laughingly calls him 'Valentino'. But D'Arcy knows better: this was no romantic flash but the sinister mark of Grey Pelt who haunts the woods and fells of their Lakeland home. And it was not the only curious thing about his appearance.

He watched mesmerised as the reflected white 'feathering' on his chest, legs and tail swayed gently with the current. Soon it would begin again. The Pack had noticed the regular change to his coat in tune with the lunar cycle. The dark ridge along his spine appeared days before the full moon, became even darker and more pronounced as the time of fullness approached then faded as Her presence diminished along with the visible face. At such times he felt the tide of his emotions swelling, and an itching of the feet that made him want to set off for he knew not where. The others had given up asking about it. Instead an uneasy stillness prevailed whenever the changes occurred, as though they knew it was something beyond themselves that D'Arcy was not allowed to share; except perhaps with his litter-sister Destiny, a fey little bitch so close to her brother they could communicate without words. Known but unspoken, the dark knowledge would cloud Destiny's eyes as she picked up his apprehension.

D'Arcy glanced up and a minute shudder rippled the blue-black hair along his spine. Twilight was creeping through the birch wood and touching with purple shadow the silver bark of the ghostly rowan trees that dotted the lower fell. He breathed in the air of late summer, honey-scented with yellow gorse and lingering lavender spikes and the loamy earthy smell of Autumn creeping through the hedgerows. A fat moon was rising above the ridge of mountains in the north. It was almost at the full and once again the Pack would become hushed and anxious. As though to emphasise this disquieting thought, a light wind breathed over the tarn rippling the surface and breaking the glassy calm. D'Arcy watched his reflection tremble then fragment beyond recognition.

At times it felt like a similar thing was happening inside his skin. A ghostly screech ripped through the silence and brought his head up sharply. *Hushwing Ghost-Owl on the hunt.* Not waiting for the next step in this all-too-familiar scenario he heaved a deep sigh and turning, made for home.

Later he was able to at least refer to it in a round-about way and so share some of the burden. Miss Tickle, blonde and curvy matron, was less aware than his sister but more so than the rest. She is Pack Nanny, you will recall, and respected Elder, and her wisdom is cloaked in simplicity.

"Are you restless tonight, D'Arcy?" she said, licking his paw in sympathy.

"I can't help it, Tickle. One day soon I shall have to go."

"But where, and for what?"

"Wherever he leads me." There was never a need to explain 'who' to Tickle; such things were understood and in any case, it didn't do to speak his name aloud.

"But in search of what?"

"I'm not sure, I think perhaps my true self."

"But what good will it do, all this searching and probing – even if you find what you seek?"

"It will make me a better Top Dog when the time comes, Tickle. Joey is getting older and we all know I am the next in line."

"But Joey does all right and he didn't go off on a Quest!" Tickle commented mildly, scratching an ear with a hind foot to pass off the awkward moment.

"No and *He* didn't visit him and mark him out!"

"That's true." Tickle's kindly face clouded with concern. "A pity he came to *you,* if you ask me! We heard the howling the night you found Destiny in the wood. He came to you just as he came to your Great Aunt Fenella; she carried the same burden."

"I need to know what he expected of Fenella. There is a reason for all this Tickle, and for the sake of the Pack's future I need to know what it is. Why does he enter one of us in each generation? What does he expect of *me*? These are the Questions I have to have answered."

"And what about Alpha-She?"

It was D'Arcy's turn to look distressed. They had a special bond, he and his Alpha. He delighted in nibbling her nose and ear and knew she understood his need and maleness and was expressing it in the only acceptable way he could. "I love her with all my heart, Tickle, and cannot bear the thought of causing her grief. But I sometimes think though she knows far more than we suspect." He recalled how she spoke in his ear the night that she heard him howling, whispering of her pride in his courage in saving his sister Destiny. It would tear him apart to leave her, even for a short while yet somehow he felt she would understand and accept. And she would wait for him and never give up on that bond. This he knew in his heart.

"When will you go?"

"I can't say Tickle. Something will happen I suppose, when the time is right."

"Will you know?"

"I guess."

"Well until then we'll put it out of our minds," Nanny Tickle said sensibly, "and we'll get a story going," she added, nudging him forward to join the rest of the pack around the Aga.

Flossie the Third

2.

How Destiny almost lost her head . . .

"Come on then, who has a good tale to tell?" Tickle demanded, wriggling her ample bottom to sit comfortably on the rug before the Aga. Destiny frowned at Tickle then gave her brother a sidelong look of warning that said: *Lady Moon is too close to the full for you to be telling stories!* She need not have worried as D'Arcy remained noticeably silent and became engrossed in removing a sprig of prickly gorse from his tail. He spat it out and returned Destiny's look with one that said *don't worry sis, I'm not about to call something up by talking about it!*

"I know, let the Little Ones have a go," Clifford piped up, lifting a front leg in the air to wave in the pups' direction so that the long 'feathering' draped in an elegant swathe of black streaked with white.

"Who? Us?" Flossie the Third and Fenella the Third chorused, whilst managing to look nervous and delighted at one and the same time. Two years had passed since their arrival as those eight-week-old babes, and until now they had been allowed to listen but not *tell* stories at the Pack Gatherings.

"What do you say Destiny?" Tickle raised eyebrows now turned white to her deputy pup-rearer.

"Okay by me Nan Tickle," Destiny agreed reluctantly, adding with a severe look for the girls, "as long as you appreciate the honour and don't get silly!"

"We won't, Aunt Destiny!" they chorused, going pink around the ears with excitement.

"So who is it to go first? You Flossie, as you are the biggest and most grown up?"

The sisters looked at one another and passed silent messages as – like D'Arcy and Destiny – they had long been in the habit of doing.

"Okay, my choice of story, Nan Tickle, but Fenella can tell it," Flossie replied with apparent generosity, opting to share with her smaller and rather naïve sister. However, Tickle raised a manicured paw to hide a little smile: more like the usually self-assured Flossie was nervous of being first to take the floor!

"I don't think so! You know Pack rules: tell your own tale, Flossie," Destiny reproved, obviously having reached the same conclusion as Tickle.

"So what tale will you be telling?" Tickle asked gently, feeling sorry for the abashed youngster.

Flossie sat up straight. "I shall tell of how Destiny nearly lost her head," she pronounced, rising to the occasion. Her ears twitched with nervousness but otherwise she hid it well.

"Oh yes, that's a good story," Tickle said nodding vigorously, but noting how Fenella sat quietly licking her paw in an effort to look unconcerned. She was, Tickle guessed, torn between relief at not having to take the floor for Flossie, and embarrassment due to her part in the story to come. Come to think of it though,

Destiny was looking uncomfortable too; maybe that was because she was the subject of the drama, but it was unusual for her to shy away from attention.

"I don't know that one," murmured Joey – a big orange lad who despite his advancing years was still the Pack's official Top Dog.

"No, it was just before you came," Clifford provided, unable to hide his satisfaction at being for once in the know where Joey was in the dark.

"No – not that one."

It was D'Arcy who had spoken, and in a tone that brooked no nonsense, and with face unusually grave.

"Choose another one, Flossie." Destiny ruled, sitting up to exchange speaking looks with her brother. Her face was taut and there was an expression in her eyes that the youngsters could not read.

"No, carry on, Flossie." Joey spoke mildly enough, but there was a strange light in his eye as he looked at D'Arcy, as though he suspected the reason behind his intervention.

"I could tell the one about finding Tilly-cat instead," Flossie offered, blinking nervously at this unexpected conflict.

"No, that is Fenella's tale for another day. As I said, I have not heard this one – and I have a mind to do so now," Joey said firmly, fixing D'Arcy with a hard look.

Destiny shrugged and lay down again and D'Arcy said no more. Joey was still Top Dog and as such had the last word.

"Come over here then, next to me and face your Pack," Destiny directed in resigned tones. Flossie did as she was bid and conscious of all eyes upon her, took a deep breath.

Well, it was all through Fenella running away . . .

(At this Fenella lowered her head, but received a nod of approval from Destiny for not letting her obvious guilt stand in the way of the story). The Pack settled and prepared to listen without interruption; they knew Flossie to be an intelligent girl who would tell it with her usual maturity and confidence now that her mind was made up.

We had all been for our daily run on the fell, Flossie began, and were ready to head back to the house. It was a Friday towards the end of April when lambs in the fields called to the mother-ewes; leaves everywhere were bursting their buds and Alpha-He was on his way home from his weekly trip to the family business. Earlier the sun had managed to slip through occasional gaps in the bank of cloud rolling in from the West, but by now had given up the struggle. A twilight of mauve and blue crept over the mountains, a soft mizzle that spangled our coats and eyelashes so that we saw everything through a rainbow haze. I started off down the fell, enjoying the lushness of tender new grass beneath my paws, then sensing the gap at my side turned to look for my sister. Fearing the worst I scanned the fell. Sure enough there was no sign of Fenella. I blinked away the drops of moisture in order to get a better look.

"Come on Pack, time to go back," Alpha-She called, making her way down through dew-spangled grass to the large wooden gate that led to the homeward path. "Flossie – hurry it up lass!" she added as I dragged behind still scanning the fell anxiously, but not wanting to get Fenella into bother. She had a reputation for escaping from the securest of places and the Alpha-Pair laughingly said she an 'ology' in it. Our Little Escapologist they called her, but her escapades were only funny in hindsight once she was safely home. Her disappearance for an hour or more over rough fell caused more distress than amusement, as did the hours spent disentangling gorse spines and brambly tendrils from her coat. The Alpha-Pair were vigilant and watched constantly to discover her escape routes, but as fast as they extended the fencing, Fenella found a way. Because of her wanderlust and disobedience, they had been forced to rule that if she escaped again, her freedom would be forfeit in favour of a long leash.

And it looked like that sis of mine had finally done it. Destiny noticed me lagging behind and dropped back to join me as the boys shot through the opening and did their usual show-off gallop along the tree-lined route to the Top Gate. Tickle had been for her Trusty run around the grounds so was not with us but snoozing in front of the Aga, otherwise she would have alerted Alpha-She at the outset. That's not to say Destiny here wasn't vigilant, you understand, it's just that Tickle has so much more experience – having had several litters of puppies to rear. Whatever, Destiny thought she could handle the situation and set off with me in tow to search for the truant. We spotted her about two thirds of the way up, still as a garden statue, front leg raised and obviously 'on point'.

Destiny called her with the sharp little bark that normally brought us running to her side (or risk a sharp nip!) and pandemonium broke lose. A terrific squawking and chuck-a-chuck-chucking split the air and a male pheasant clattered up, wings flapping and cracking in front of us. I darted forward as Fenella leapt up high and managed to reach the top of the fence, where she hung by her forepaws. Destiny loosed a warning volley of barks as Fenella used the leverage of her front legs to scrabble like mad with the rear ones, until she flopped over the top of the fence with a plop into the long grass.

"Defiant little bitch!" Destiny snapped and temper up, ran at the fence and stuck her head through a gap near the bottom. "Get back here, like now – or I chew your ears off!" she barked, but Fenella, oblivious to the tirade, was already bounding after the pheasant and was soon out of sight.

"You know what your sister's like – why didn't you keep an eye on her?" Destiny demanded, her head whipping round to glare at me as she pulled back. "She's gone, Destiny," I said dolefully, knowing Alpha-She would be distraught, and Alpha-He's home-coming once again spoiled by trauma.

"There's nothing we can do here; let's go back and alert Alpha-She."

"I can't."

That was all she said. Yet my stomach churned at the quiet panic behind the words. In my distress I had failed to notice that Destiny's head was now stuck at an odd angle. In turning quickly she had twisted the wire and the more she struggled the tighter it became.

"Destiny!" I didn't know what to do and felt sick with fear as she began threshing about in panic, growling and snarling to vent her fear and frustration. Then the growling became a strangled moan as the wire bit into her throat and Destiny dropped to the ground, her head yanked up at that unnatural angle.

"What can I do, Destiny?" I pleaded, licking her face to give comfort. Destiny opened her mouth to speak but only a hoarse whisper came out. Her breath was coming in painful gasps and I yelped with fear as blood trickled down her throat and onto her chest. As though sensing this, and the dire state she was in, Destiny began threshing about once more, making the situation worse. "Tell me what to do!" I barked in a frenzy, unable to think for myself. Then instinct took over, and dropping onto my haunches beside her I tried to grasp the wire with my teeth. It was too tight for me to get a hold and she flinched as my teeth nipped the skin.

"Be still Destiny!" I barked, "you have to stay still," I yelled as the wire bit deeper. Her tongue lolled out from the side of her mouth and her eyes were becoming glazed and of necessity she lay still and spent. Heart thumping and legs turning to jelly I tried to clear the fog of panic from my head. I had to do something before it was too late. But what? It was unthinkable to leave her here alone and in this condition. I shuddered to think of returning to find her limp and cold, and knowing she had died on this fell-side all alone. It seemed all I could do was lie down beside her so that she did not die alone.

It would not do! My heart and mind rebelled against the idea of just giving her up without a fight. I had to get Fenella back. I sat bolt upright and barked so loud my front paws left the ground with each volley, so great was the effort. At last I heard a rustling through the long grass and my nostrils twitched at the scent of my sister.

"I'm here, what's the sweat? You knew I'd . . ." Fenella bounded up breathlessly, then stopped dead in mid-sentence on seeing Destiny's plight, "Oh Great Mother-in-the-Sky, what happened?"

"You did!" I couldn't help snapping, but then realised that recriminations were a waste of precious minutes. "I have to go and get help, you must stay with her and keep her in there Fenella."

The terrible sound of Destiny's struggle to breathe tore at our hearts. Panic stabbed my chest as the threshing became less and less and her limbs sank limply to the ground.

"How? What do I do? Don't leave me here with her Flossie, I'm scared!"

Fenella's eyes were starting in fear and clouded with guilt, and saliva dribbled from her mouth. At that moment she looked like the baby she in spirit still was. I hesitated a second: apart from Clifford, Fenella was the swiftest member of our Pack. Maybe she should go. But she was also a bit of a flibberty jibbet and could I trust her to find Alpha if she wasn't at the house? No, I had to be the one to go.

"You should have thought of that before going AWOL. Now talk to her, lick her face and at all costs, keep her awake. Lie down next to her and don't move!"

Subdued and silent, Fenella sank onto her belly.

I bent over Destiny, terrified by the tearing sound of the breath in her throat and the blood-flecked foam that now dotted her mouth. "I'm going to get help Destiny!" I panted, licking her nose and mouth clean, "I'll be back with Alpha-She. We'll have you free in no time, you'll see."

25

I struggled to hide my fear and distress as her eyes pleaded with me not to leave, then rolled back in her head.

"Stay with me, Flossie," she managed to croak. I leaned closer, struggling to make out the words as she panted and fought for air. "I'm done for, please don't leave me alone! Just wait with me until it is over."

"No! Don't say that!" I yelped.

"There are things you must know. You are next in line and must be able to take over from me," she croaked, ignoring my plea. My heart leapt as her limbs began to jerk uncontrollably. "Talk to me about Ben," she gasped, as though realising it was too late for instruction or anything else. "Tell me how he will be waiting for me at the Rainbow Bridge when it happens," she whispered almost inaudibly. I felt the waves of her fear and panic beating against my skin.

I hesitated – torn in two by my dilemma. If I left her now and she died in my absence I would not be able to live with myself. But if I didn't run for help any slight chance of saving Destiny would be lost.

"Don't die, Destiny. We can't go on without you!" I whimpered. A prompt decision was vital, but panic clouded my brain, making me quake and dither.

I was young, inexperienced – and frightened half to death.

In that tortuous moment I looked at my little sister without knowing why. The skin along my spine prickled as the mask on her face seemed to grow blacker, her coat more luxurious and her eyes larger and more oval, her stature more imposing. I struggled with a lost memory, then realised with a jolt that she was the image of a picture on the wall back at the house. Our Great Aunt Fenella the Second stared back at me. Destiny was scarcely breathing now, her body limp and still and her eyes were glazing over. She was close to her time. I began to shiver, terrified by what was happening here, of what I could not understand. I wanted to flee in panic yet stay and rouse her at the same time. Whilst I dithered, Fenella drew herself up to give me a yellow-eyed stare that sent fresh shivers along my spine. Her mouth opened as though in slow motion and one word was spit from the depths: "Go!" she hissed.

I knew better than to argue. I lowered my head and licked Destiny's muzzle, secretly thankful that the decision was made for me. "I'm going for Alpha now Destiny – we'll save you, don't worry," I whispered hoarsely.

The look she gave me before I turned on the spot and raced for the gate broke my heart.

On reaching it I turned and looked back. My breath caught in my throat at the sight of Fenella the Third standing with tail erect, head raised to the darkening sky and mouth agape. From its depths bubbled a strange and haunting wail that tugged at my soul and the strings of memory. I had seen enough. Terror stricken, I turned and fled. The mournful cry hovered on the twilight air, thin and ancient and swelling in volume even as I listened. It still sang in my ears as I fled along the tree-lined path to the End Gate.

My prayers that it would still be open were answered. I sped through and on and up under the tree canopy, past the old Nissan Hut and on to the next gate, panting and struggling for breath, and running as I had never run before. Destiny's life depended upon me finding Alpha in time and not only that, but making her understand. An impossible task with less than minutes to spare. At least Fenella's howling was holding Destiny's attention and keeping her there, giving me precious time. Yet, even as I ran, I knew there was more to it: in my soul I knew she was summoning help of a nature I could not understand but which nevertheless was real.

Panting and with foam-flecked muzzle I raced into the compound and tried to bark with what breath remained. Despite the pathetic gasping that emerged the door opened and Alpha-She stood on the threshold. I closed my mouth and watched in awe.

There was something strange about her expression: the far-away look in her eyes and the way she tilted her head as though to listen. I could hear nothing now except the stirring of leaves in the evening breeze.

"What is it, Flossie? Who is hurt?" she said immediately, her voice strained and strangely quiet. I barked to tell her it was Destiny and that every second counted. There was no need, she was already at the gate. But it was no use without the means to free Destiny. I threw my paws against the mesh of the pen, then as she watched frowning and clearly not understanding, I did it again but then stood and growled, snarled and barked at the fence. I saw the light of maybe-understanding dawning. She disappeared into the house and came back with pliers and pair of wire snips in hand.

"I may be wrong, Flossie, but we might just need these."

I barked with excitement and ran to the gate to show she had it right.

Having got my breath back I had to rein in my impatience and stop myself from tearing ahead. *Are we in time? Is Destiny still alive?* These Questions tortured me and yet drove me on. My limbs itched to tear on ahead but I had to lead Alpha to the spot. She ran like the wind, chest heaving and breath gasping but the pace was taking its toll. There was a grimace of pain on her face and the free hand flew briefly to her side, but she carried on punching the air and driving herself onward. Terrible pictures arose in my mind, of Destiny lying still and lifeless on the ground and I knew I must prepare myself for the worst. She could not survive this long, I told myself, she had been close to death even before I left.

At last we were on the fell and I barked as I ran: "Destiny, Destiny, are you still with us?" There was no reply. Alpha-She stumbled after me, the slope slowing her down and demanding ever more effort as we climbed. My heart lurched in my chest as Destiny came into sight. She lay without moving, and Fenella

28

was lying by her side, also immobile, energy spent. *Oh, Great Mother, we are too late,* I sobbed to myself, rushing to Destiny's still form. I heard Alpha's distraught cry and felt the waves of anguish at my back. I had failed. How could I live with myself now? How could the Pack survive without our beloved, feisty Destiny? I dropped down by her side, spirit crushed and unable to grasp that she had really gone.

Destiny at the scene of her ordeal

3.

Flossie's tale has repercussions . . .

Alpha-She dropped to her knees and stroked Destiny's head.

"I'm here, Destiny, I'm here," she whispered, tears dripping onto Destiny's head as she felt her motionless body.

"There's still a pulse!" Alpha-She cried. "Quick! Got to be quick!" she exhorted herself, and dropping pincers to the ground she took the cutters to the wire. It was no use, there was not enough slack to insert the blade without the risk of cutting flesh. She murmured encouragement to Destiny as she worked, then dropped the cutters in exasperation. Picking up the pliers she clamped them onto the adjoining wire and tugged with all her might. A weak whimper escaped Destiny but Alpha remained focused. "I may have to hurt you to save your life, Dezzy," she hissed, her face turning from shock-induced white to red with effort. At last the tension caused the section of wire around Destiny's neck to give a fraction.

Quick as a flash Alpha-She slipped in the pliers and tugged. This was live-stock fencing and tough, and Alpha's slight wrists were no match for it. Moaning with pain and frustration, veins on the back of her hands raised and contorted, she squeezed and pulled again and gained a few centimeters. Destiny's neck was now free of the wire but during the attempt to release the pressure, the vertical opening had moved lengthwise to form a buckled and flattened rectangle, leaving no room to pull her head through. Panting from exertion Alpha sat back on her heels and weighed up the situation. Destiny was weakening, there was no time to lose. "I have to do this, Destiny," she muttered under her breath, whilst clasping Destiny's neck with one hand and a shoulder with the other. A pause, whilst Fenella and I held our breath; we guessed what Alpha was about to do, and if it went wrong, it meant a broken neck and curtains. "Now!" Alpha cried. A quick twist and Destiny was flipped onto her side. Her head was now aligned with the opening. Alpha laid a hand along her flank in a quick check, "She's still breathing!" We sighed with relief then held our breath again as the operation to free her continued. Taking a deep breath, Alpha grasped Destiny's neck and began to manoeuver her backwards. As her head appeared in the gap she cradled it in one hand and guided it into line and tugged against the resistance. We watched Alpha's lips moving in a silent prayer as she appeared to make up mind. Then one quick wrench and Destiny was free.

Destiny lay on the grass, her body and limbs limp and unmoving. Alpha-She bent over her still form and rhythmically massaged her chest
"She's in shock," she said tersely. "Back girls – stand back and give her some space."
Obediently we backed off a pace but jostled each other and craned our necks to see. The minutes passed without response and our hearts sank. But suddenly Destiny's chest rose and fell on a shuddering sigh. Her eyes opened and she gazed into her Alpha's face with dazed expression.

"It's all right, Destiny," Alpha soothed, pulling her close and cradling her in her arms. They remained like that for several minutes, knowing that anything else could wait. I swear I could feel Alpha's energy flowing into Destiny's still form. We hung back, wanting to let Destiny know we were there for her but afraid to intrude.

"Come and say hello to your Aunt Destiny." Sensing our confusion and distress Alpha smiled through her tears and beckoned us forward. We licked Destiny's face and snuffled her ears, letting her know how glad we were that she had come back to us.

"Alpha-He should be back by now. You wait here Destiny and we'll get him to carry you home. Then tomorrow he can check all the fences for repairs."

Destiny's anxious expression and somewhat croaky bark said 'not likely, I'm coming with you!' A few minutes later she staggered to her feet but then flopped down again immediately.

"No, Destiny, I'll fetch help," Alpha-She said firmly, but determined not to be left again, Destiny was already struggling upright. She remained like that for several minutes, watched anxiously by the rest of us as she flexed her muscles, tested the feel of her pads against the ground and gathered her wits. Then she slowly moved forward to lick first my face then Fenella's to thank us for our part in her rescue. Apart from swaying from side to side with weakness, and wearing a jagged red line around her throat, she was apparently none the worse for her adventure.

"Let's get you all home and Destiny doctored." Alpha led the way down the fell at a slow pace, through the Fell Gate, along the Home Path and into the warm and welcoming kitchen.

My sister and I couldn't get to sleep that night for whispering about Destiny's adventure, yet strangely neither of us mentioned the change that had briefly overcome Fenella. It was to be many nights before we felt able to go there, and eventually when we did speak, it was in hushed tones.

"What happened to you sis?" I asked one night as we lay on our beds in the separate little room off the kitchen. We had to whisper because the top part of the stable-type door was always left often so that the warmth from the Aga filtered through to keep us snug and we were not cut off from the Pack. The rest of you were just the other side of course, and would have overhead had we not kept our voices low.

"I don't know. I felt peculiar like I was still myself, but somebody else as well," Fenella replied in a voice so low I could only just hear.

"Like how?"

"It was like I'd been here before: pictures in my head and feelings in my body of things I only half recognised, you know, vague memories like when you try to remember a dream."

"Pictures of what though?"

"The mountain at twilight flashing by as though I was running . . ."

"You were!" I couldn't resist the jibe.

"That was before Destiny got stuck!"

"Okay, go on."

"Well stop messing or I go to sleep."

"Excuse me little sis! What else then?"

"I felt a long, mournful sound bubbling up in me and I had to let it go."

"We all heard – including Alpha-She! And?"

"I could taste the wind and big spaces and I felt big too!"

"What do you mean?"

"Like the rest of me had grown into my feet!"

I had to smile when she told me this, but it was scary too. You all know Nanny Tickle's tale of how the Great Mother made the Big Girl's feet again, but because Fenella the Second was too busy flitting amongst the stars and didn't get back in time, there wasn't enough energy left to match her new body to her feet! So this time round, Fenella the Third – my sister – has big feet but the rest of her is tiny! We all loved that story but I for one didn't

33

really think it happened that way, not until that night. I mean, here she is telling me it is for real. Scary stuff, I think you'll agree. Anyway, I tried asking more questions but she wasn't for giving answers.

"When did you go back to your ordinary size?" I asked.

"You're making my head hurt," Fenella grumbled. Tucking her nose into her flank, she curled up ready for sleep. I knew there was no point in pushing further; she wasn't about to tell. I guessed we must all be grateful for Destiny's rescue and not question what it was not our place to know.

"And that, Flossie concluded looking around self-consciously at her audience, is how Destiny almost lost her head."

"That was a splendid story and well told!" Nanny Tickle exclaimed, nodding in approval.

"Yes, well done youngster," Joey growled, blinking rapidly to show his pleasure.

Tickle turned to Fenella and patted her forepaw. "I reckon your Great Aunt Fenella came through to help you, Little One."

A remark that was greeted with the solemn silence of the half-understood.

"It was brill," Clifford enthused to change the mood. He waved his paw in the air to emphasise the point. "Wasn't it, D'Arcy?"

"H'm'm'm."

"What is it, mate?"

"Nothing." D'Arcy shook his head as though to banish the frown that creased his forehead. "No, it was good, real good. Well done Flossie," he added, then shot his sister an anxious look. Destiny was staring at him with a strange expression on her face.

"Have I got something wrong?" Flossie asked, crestfallen.

"Not at all," Destiny said turning from her brother to Flossie. "You did well, especially as it was your first Telling."

34

"Thank you." Flossie sat upright and kept silence, but her whiskers quivered revealing her intense pleasure.

"In fact," Destiny added with a strange look for her brother, "it was so good I can almost hear an answering call, a summons from One-who-cannot-be-named!"

The applause that had broken out trickled into the uncomfortable silence that follows the broaching of a taboo.

Miss Tickle broke it and provided a diversion by producing half a soggy chew stick. "I saved this to have in my bed tonight," she confessed, "but I think the teller of such a tale deserves a reward! Come forward and claim it Flossie," she said grandly, grasping the prize in her teeth. Glowing pink around the gills Flossie accepted it and lying down held it between her forepaws and began to munch. Fenella looked on, trying not to look envious.

"I think your sister did well in that story too. Despite being the cause, she redeemed herself in the end." It was Destiny who had spoken, and again she threw a look at her brother that none could fully understand.

"I'll save you some Fen," Flossie said graciously, nodding at her sister who wagged her tail in anticipation.

"But we don't know how you felt, Aunt Destiny," Fenella said shyly. "How did it feel to be so close to death?"

"Dear me, what a thing to ask!" murmured Nanny Tickle, shaking her head. "Hush Little One, do!"

"No, it's good that she has thought about this and wants to know such things," Destiny intervened. "At first it was all pain and fear, but as I grew weaker it was like Grandsire Ben was there by my side. Next thing I knew I was standing at the foot of a sandstone cliff on the shores of a sunlit lake with delicate trees dipping and swaying on either side. I remember slow-moving ripples rimmed with sunlight that slid into shore and over my feet, making me feel warm and calm. It felt like Alpha-She's love."

Destiny fell silent then and there spread across her features the dreamy, far-away expression they knew so well.

"Then Alpha-She came," Destiny continued, and the far-off expression faded as she returned to them. "I knew she was there but couldn't struggle back from that sunlit shore. Then I heard her call to me and felt her distress, and also her life-force flowing into my body. I saw it shudder and my eyes open, and suddenly was back inside it again."

"What did that feel like?" Flossie asked, ever curious.

"Like nothing. No rushing wind or flying through the air or anything so dramatic! One minute I was on the shore of the lake, the next I was back on the grass with my head stuck through that stupid fence!" she said lightly, as though to buffer the gravity of this turn in the conversation. "I began to feel pain again, but only for a short time and was glad I could, I can tell you! The rest you know," she added.

"I was so relieved, sis," D'Arcy murmured over the restrained laughter that followed this. "I can't imagine being without you."

"You'll do well to remember that, bro."

Destiny swiftly covered up her sharpness by turning to Flossie and saying jokingly "Well done, youngster. I'd best watch out, or you'll be ousting me as Pack Poet next!"

Flossie and Fenella giggled together and looked embarrassed but hugely pleased. D'Arcy remained silent amidst the youngsters' confusion and pack laughter, and Tickle's heart hurt to see the look of sadness on her darling boy's face.

Later that night when the Pack were chatting companionably together, winding down ready for supper and bed, D'Arcy joined his sister who had gone outside alone. She stood motionless, gazing out at the stars.

"Don't do it, Desty," he said quietly, moving forward to stand at her side.

"That's my line I think!" Her voice was sharp, her expression cool.

"I'm not deliberately hurting you."

"You will."

36

"Stop playing games, Destiny. I want it to be like it was – we were so close you and me."

"It's not me that wants to move away."

"Neither do I Des. I'm being torn apart."

"Sure." Destiny's lip curled in a brittle smile. "I'm only concerned for the others. Don't fret on my behalf D'Arcy, you can leave tonight for all I care."

D'Arcy winced as though she had physically wounded him and he sighed and walked to the door. Had he turned around then, he would have seen a world of hurt and confusion in his sister's eyes.

Ben: Poor D'Arcy. He knows what must lie ahead and already knows the pain of almost losing his sister. But I could not have let Destiny perish out there on the fell. My heart went out to those youngsters, lost in the tragedy of their own making. Yet I knew Fenella would redeem herself through inborn courage and allegiance to her lineage, one she had no idea she possessed. As for Destiny, yes I bore her away to that sunlit shore far from her pain and distress. Clear waters lapped her feet and bathed them in hope. She stood there, basking in the warmth and peace of eternal sunlight, silently calling to her Alpha. And through me, and Alpha-She's deep and abiding love, that cry was heard. This I could do; but actually save her from Fenella's folly I could not; that task was allotted to Flossie and Alpha-She in order that they too might learn and grow.

You see in many ways this new world in which I find myself is similar to your own. I do have some modest new abilities yes, but only those I have earned during my time here; I am a novice still so these powers are limited. On first arriving here our light is as insignificant as a far-off star in a vast night-sky, but as we develop and nourish a desire to help those left behind, it grows bigger, glows brighter and can penetrate further. Those souls that have been here long and learned much, shine brighter than the largest planets and we cannot look at them directly. They are like archangels, and closest to the Great Mother of Us All. When I first crossed the bridge I should not have been able to do anything at all, but my immense love for Alpha-She enabled me to paint a rainbow in her sky or leave her a white angel-feather in an unlikely place when her grief became too great. Love is the key that opens doors and helps us do things beyond our normal powers. A lesson learnt by both Flossie and Fenella during this adventure, and confirmed for Alpha-She. Now the Pack must learn the hardest lesson of all: that sometimes we have to let go, at least, for a time . . .

Joey has something important to say

4.

Beginnings . . .

Over the following nights Lady Moon swelled to a golden globe and D'Arcy writhed on his bed as he lay sleepless. The dark ridge rippling his back was even more marked than usual, and his bones ached as though cramped within his body as they stretched and elongated whilst lacking the space to grow. Destiny watched him from under white lashes. Her hazel eyes, slanted in watchfulness and flecked with the green of a slatey pool, gave nothing away. During the times when he did manage to sleep, D'Arcy groaned and his feet twitched frantically as though running to or from something awesome.

The full moon sent beams of silver streaming in through the window and onto his bed. The ache in his spine and limbs grew sharper, compelling him to move. Rising from his bed he padded to the stable-type door and found the bottom section was open.

Passing through into the kitchen he moved silently to the outer door and into the night. After the warmth of the den, the already cooling air of a pre-Autumn night shocked his nostrils, that and the sharp scent of pine mingled with the loamy smell of the earth beneath the broadleaf copse. The time was drawing near. His nostrils twitched; there was an underlying primeval odour that made the dark ridge of hair along his spine ripple and quiver with recognition. He stood motionless, listening to the rustle of mouse, vole, and the occasional hedge-pig through the undergrowth and tall grass at the edge of the copse. A bloodcurdling screech froze him in his tracks. The white shape sailed over the treetops, so low that the wing tips almost brushed the uppermost branches. *Hushwing Ghost-Owl.* This time there was no accompanying shiver of fear, only a quiver of acknowledgement and an urge to throw back his head and return the greeting. The untimely impulse was stifled, and body slung low to ground he slinked away from the sleeping house, through the shadowed garden and onto the moonlit fell.

He paused half-way and gazed up at the black crag of the summit etched against the great golden globe. As he watched a dark shape moved forward and stood motionless, silhouetted against the full moon. D'Arcy's feet impelled him forward of their own volition. He moved faster now, more surely and with longer stride and greater confidence in a strength borrowed from his ancestors. As he approached the great head was drawn back and the jaws opened ready to loose the howl. D'Arcy moved alongside, mapping his stance to that of the other. A gleam of yellow eye and the first haunting note bubbling in the creature's throat caused the fragile boundary of skin and bone to melt. He felt himself flowing into the other's body, and the surge of an awesome power. Limbs and body quivering he tilted his head and the power pried open his jaws, willing him to bay his homage to the Female Goddess in her guise of Lady Moon. The first thin wailing cry struggled to be born from the depths of his soul and trembled in his throat.

"D'Arcy!"

The sharp sound of his name being called collided with the burgeoning wail and sent him shuddering back into his own body.

"D'Arcy, what is it?"

He blinked in the sudden glare as the kitchen lamp was switched on. Alpha-She stood looking in at him, an expression of consternation on her face. Dazed and confused he stared at his beloved Alpha, then opened and closed his eyes twice to let her know that there was no longer cause for concern. She gave him a long look, talking to him with her eyes, telling him that she understood and giving him reassurance.

"It's hard for you, D'Arcy, I know," she whispered, "It was like that with your Great Aunt Fenella too. You must fight it and not give in to the call." As she leaned close to whisper again he saw the tears trembling on her lashes. "I couldn't bear to lose you, Darling Boy," she murmured, and his heart filled with a love and pain so intense he could scarcely breathe. He gave her a look that mirrored her devotion and she nodded and left him then.

"Are you all right D'Arcy?"

He blinked and looked round at the others who were sitting up and looking at him with equal concern. It was Clifford who had spoken and the love of Alpha and the pack broke through the remaining layers of enchantment and shattered his moon-struck state. He began to shudder and shake with realization of what had taken place.

"Hold it together, mate; we're all here for you." It was Joey this time who sought to reassure, and his big handsome face crinkled with the worry of what he could not understand.

"What happened, dear boy?" Tickle moved from her bed to snuggle up next to him, giving him warmth and comfort.

"I went out into the garden, then onto the fell and – well, I wasn't myself," he faltered and finished lamely, aware that in his need for support he had almost said too much.

41

Destiny stirred on her bed and shook her head in denial. "No. You couldn't have done."

"But I did go out . . ." he started to protest.

"Look," she said, pointing with a forepaw.

"But I tell you I . . ." then he saw where she was pointing and fell silent.

"That's right, the bottom half of the door is shut," Destiny added, "you were dreaming, bro."

He nodded. "You must be right, sis."

With a deep sigh he allowed his tense muscles to relax and lowered his head to sleep, aware of Tickle's warm nanny body at his back – and his sister's watchful eye upon him. But he was also conscious of the dampness of his pads and the droplets of dew that spangled his feathers.

Then something happened to focus his intent. A week or so later they were all in the meadow, the youngsters playing and exploring whilst the elders basked in the mellowing sunlight. The wildflowers were now turning to seed or like the Aquilegia – or Grandmother's Bonnet as Tickle called it, preferring the old country name – had already popped their pods to scatter their seeds abroad. Ox-eye daisies still starred the green, and some late-flowering foxgloves sported pink or white flowers on their now sparsely-populated spikes. Tickle, content these days to snooze in the sun, breathed in the scent of warm ripe apples and the sweet smell of blackberries from the hedgerow. Joey was relaxing in his favourite spot on the grassy plateau, a vantage point from which he could either dream along with the misty mountains or keep a watchful eye on his pack.

Puffed from chasing the younger girls, D'Arcy flopped down beside him, tongue lolling and flanks heaving.

"Take some catching those young 'uns," Joey commented in friendly fashion.

"Doesn't do to let them know it though!" D'Arcy grinned as beads of saliva dripped from his tongue and sparkled on a blade of foxtail grass.

"We're none of us getting any younger."

Something in Joey's tone made D'Arcy pause in his panting and give him a speculative look. "Plenty of life in you yet though, eh Joey?"

"You have many years ahead of you D'Arcy."

"You too, Joey! So have you." And D'Arcy tried to keep the need for reassurance out of his voice.

Joey watched a late dragonfly whirring overhead in the direction of Merlins Mere on a desperate last-minute mission to find a mate. D'Arcy frowned and put his head to one side, surveying Joey. Was he misreading something here, was the big boy trying to tell him something? "Everything is all right, isn't it mate?" he asked, not liking Joey's far-away look and air of detachment.

"You need to decide soon D'Arcy."

"I don't know what you mean!" D'Arcy blustered unable to meet Joey's eye.

"If you are determined to go, then you must make it soon."

D'Arcy opened his mouth to protest then realised there was little point in denial.

"How come you know?"

"That doesn't matter." Joey gave a big sigh as though suddenly weary. "Just make up your mind, and if you decide on this Quest then go sooner rather than later."

"I know, Autumn is coming on and I have to go before Winter sets in."

Something in Joey's expression caused D'Arcy to fall silent. A cold hand seemed to reach inside his chest and lay icy fingers around his heart. "But you are fit, mate," he whispered.

Joey gave him a penetrating look and didn't answer directly. "I'm getting tired D'Arcy. And there is something not quite right . . ."

"We'll let Alpha-She know – she'll get you put right," D'Arcy said eagerly, hope flaring in his eyes.

"It's too late for that D'Arcy. And listen to me carefully now — you say nothing to anyone, do you understand? Especially not to Tickle. I have some time left and I am going to be sure she enjoys our last days together, so don't you go making her sad! As for Alpha-She, her instinct will kick in soon enough and she will know the truth and be there for me, I have no fear about that. So promise me you will stay silent."

"You cannot ask this of me Joey!"

"I can and have. Who else can I trust with this other than my successor?"

D'Arcy stared at him miserably. The thing he had coveted so long was now the last thing on earth he wanted to possess.

"I am not in any pain and when the time comes it will be quick," Joey soothed, reading his underling's expression.

"But how do you know? You could be mistaken!"

"Ben comes to me these days. He has prepared me. I shall be going home with my father, so I'm not sad or afraid. We shall all be together again in time; I'm simply going on ahead of you all."

D'Arcy's heart sunk into his stomach. *Ben.* This omen he could not argue against.

"No, I don't want you to go!" Suddenly the big bold next-in-command became the lost and bewildered youngster.

"I am eleven years old D'Arcy," Joey said gently. "Let's have no false sadness. I've had the best life any dog could wish for, and the best pack too!"

"I'm not going anywhere now, how can I? What do you take me for Joe?"

"A dog with a mission. I've told you, there is still time. I don't really understand it, but if this Quest makes a better Top Dog of you when I'm gone, then you have my blessing. Don't hesitate too long is all I am saying, the pack will need you when my time comes. And remember . . . not a word. Promise me, D'Arcy. Give me your word on it," he insisted when D'Arcy remained silent.

"If I must. Though it's a heavy burden to carry."

"It goes with the job matey!"

"I guess." Seeing Joey's lop-sided grin D'Arcy felt more cheerful and decided the big lad was right; if there was truth in what he said then there was nothing to be done about it, but nothing to fear either. And they might as well enjoy the time he had left. Besides, he comforted himself, Joey may well have it all wrong.

Nevertheless, that conversation weighed heavily on his shoulders. He found himself watching Joey surreptitiously, then he would glance away when the others began to notice. Outwardly, Joey seemed his normal self, and if he slept more these days, well, as Joey had stated, he was eleven years of age and so this could be expected. He still carried out his duties impeccably and kept control of his pack, not by any visible show but by that quiet air of authority that all recognised and instinctively obeyed. A legacy from Ben, D'Arcy realised, secretly worrying about whether he would develop his grandsire's dignity and leader's presence. Ben was the archetype Top Dog, whereas Joey was a gentler, laid-back and perhaps kinder leader. Joey's style will be my approach, D'Arcy realised, with some insight into his own generous and easy-going nature. Not wanting to go there, he dismissed the thought as swiftly as it had come and trotted over to lie next to Destiny in an effort to melt her recent frostiness.

As the next full moon approached and the familiar scenario of changed appearance and disquieting urges loomed, D'Arcy spent restless nights thinking things through and in laying tentative plans. It made no odds really, he decided, whether Joey was right or wrong; he *was* getting older and to go absent in his twelfth, thirteenth or hopefully even later years was not on. If at all, it had to be now. At the very least Joey would need a good deputy to rely on, and the pack assurances of continuity with a future leader. He had almost decided to leave it to nature and follow the urges as they occurred when something happened to disrupt the pack and prevent him putting this plan into action.

Pippa joins the Pack

5.

Alpha-She springs a surprise

On a day when the sun set foliage of red, orange and gold alight and melted the first faint traces of white from the garden, Alpha-She got into her car and drove away leaving them in Alpha-He's care. There were treats a-plenty, rules were relaxed and they played till the sun went down but D'Arcy could not settle. Whilst the others enjoyed their day of freedom under Alpha-He's indulgent eye, D'Arcy constantly put up his head and sniffed the air, and watched the lane from the fell run, anxiously awaiting the sound and smell of Alpha-She's car. Night fell and still there was no sign of Alpha-She's return. It was so unlike her to stay away from them overnight, he worried, hiding his anxiety from Joey's suspicious gaze and deflecting Destiny's inquisitive probing. It had to be something important; she never left her pack unless strictly necessary as she missed them all every bit as much as they missed her, but in his heart he knew she missed him, her first boy, more than any.

The following day D'Arcy leapt up onto the settle by the Aga, startling the other pack members by barking loud and from deep within his belly.

"What's the matter with you, bro? You made me pee on the floor with fright!" Destiny fibbed.

"Scared me too, but I didn't pee, honest!" Clifford looked down at the floor with a worried frown, wondering if he would get the blame; he was notorious for leaving his mark whenever one of the little girls was in season.

"And we're not coming into season, we finished last month," Flossie declared with an indignant frown; the girls sometimes had 'accidents' around this time.

"Don't be silly Clifford, Flossie – she didn't really, it was just an expression," Nanny Tickle said sensibly, whilst Destiny sat straight up on the settle and rolled her eyes to the ceiling.

D'Arcy ignored all this banter and started barking again. Before any of the others had realised, he heard the sound of Alpha-She's car returning.

"Come say hello to Pippa."

Alpha-She stood in the kitchen doorway, breaking her silence, making eye-contact and greeting them each in turn only after the pack had settled down from their excitement at her return. They scuttled in her wake, trying to contain their glee at her return, as she led the way to back door.

"Didn't you bring her in with you?" Alpha-He asked, looking puzzled.

Alpha-She shook her head. "That would be bringing her into the heart of their territory uninvited. To be accepted into the pack they must invite her in and she must follow."

"I see. Well, this should be fun!"

Alpha-She opened the door and led the way into the pen.

As the boys led by Joey raced out with the girls at their tails, the little blue bitch sitting on the centre flagstone rose and shook

47

her feathers. Looking slightly puzzled about where she was and why but totally unafraid, she allowed the boys to sniff enthusiastically around her tail.

"No problem there," Alpha-He commented with a nod and a smile.

"Not surprising," Alpha-She said dryly. "She's only four, and pretty with it! That black eye-patch gives her a distinctly roguish look!"

"She"ll fit in all right," Alpha-He said smiling.

"Oh, she'll win you and the boys over all right, it's the girls we have to worry about!" Alpha-She gestured at Destiny who was standing stock still, tail raised and guarding Flossie and Fenella with her body. Alpha-She walked towards Pippa and reaching out, stroked her head once or twice whilst staring Destiny in the eye. "Pippa has been poorly, so Be Kind!" she said quietly but firmly before retreating to her previous position by the door.

"Hello, Pippa, and welcome to the Pack." It was Nanny Tickle who moved forward to break the uncomfortable silence.

Destiny bridled as Flossie and Fenella started to move towards the newcomer, and immediately they froze.

"Come on girls, say hello," Tickle said brightly, ignoring Destiny's hard stare and rigid body.

The two youngest girls looked uneasily at one another then at Destiny who glared back at them, but in response to Tickle's prompting, the youngsters ran forward to eye and sniff the new arrival.

"Hi Pippa, I'm Flossie the Third."

"And I'm Fenella the Third, but you can call us Flossie and Fenella," her sister said ever-generous, tempering Flossie's slightly pompous tone and bearing.

They both fell back as one as Destiny's shadow fell over the three of them.

"And I'm Destiny, and you can call me Top Bitch," she growled.

"Destiny!" Alpha-He warned, but Alpha-She took his arm and ushered him indoors. "They have to be left to sort it for themselves," she said leading him inside to watch from the kitchen window. "Pippa has to find her place in the pack hierarchy, and Destiny has to establish her authority but at the same time accept her into the pack."

Alpha-He looked a trifle anxious. "How do you know she will?"

"Because I touched Pippa, giving out the message that I accept her so they must too," Alpha-She said simply. "And no matter how feisty, Destiny has to obey her Alpha. She understands what I mean by 'be kind' too."

"That's pretty cool, but she doesn't look to be in too much of a hurry to conform!"

"She's just making sure Pippa knows the score! Destiny is nobody's fool: she's picked up already that Pippa is used to being top bitch at her kennels and will try to retain that position here. So this should be interesting!"

Alpha-She's eyes twinkled as she turned back to watch the scenario being played out beyond the kitchen window.

"So what about these allergies?" There was concern in Alpha-He's voice.

"Don't worry: The whole idea is that the change of environment and regime will make the difference but we must wait and see."

"I hope you are right. She's a bonny little bitch, I think I'd like her to stay," Alpha-He said casually, busying himself with filling the kettle and placing it on the Aga hot plate.

Not fooled for a moment, Alpha-She smiled to herself and nodded. It was obvious that Pippa had already won one heart in her new home. It was to be hoped she managed at least to win Destiny's forbearance. From the events taking place outside the window, it seemed fairly certain that Pippa would have an uphill struggle in this respect.

"So what you doing here?" Destiny demanded, tail raised and bristling.

Pippa shrugged and tried to look unfazed by this thinly-veiled challenge.

"Like Alpha-She said, I wasn't well."

"Okay, but why come to us?"

"Because she will get better here with us to help her, so leave her be Destiny!"

It was Tickle who had spoken, with a stomping of her front paw to underline each word. This was the Nanny Tickle who stood no nonsense from her charges, the Tickle they rarely saw these days but still respected – and obeyed.

Destiny whirled round to face her, tail stiff as a ramrod, eyes staring and hard. For several breath-stopping moments she held Tickle's gaze without flinching, then reading something there, dropped it, shrugged and turned away.

All but Destiny and Fenella welcomed the newcomer into the pack: Destiny for an obvious and partly valid reason; and little Fenella in the hope of rising above her lowly but important Omega rank of Peacemaker by forcing Pippa to take it instead. But Pippa was a mature four-year-old with other ideas and all Fenella's prancing and nudging – in fair imitation of her Aunt Destiny's tactics – were of little effect. Then came a June day when the pollen was high on the Meadow Run and on their return Pippa's eyes streamed and her ears turned red and she suffered much distress. Kindly little Fenella was instantly sorry and despite warning looks, left Destiny's side to lick Pippa's ears in an attempt to cool them.

"Good girl, Fenella; I'll sort it now," Alpha-She said, reaching for a cooling spray.

From that day on Pippa had a small but loyal new friend. Before long Flossie joined her sister. Ever on the ball, Destiny quickly realised that if she was to keep the loyalty of the girls there was no alternative but to accept the newcomer. It may have been coincidence, but Pippa's coat grew thick and long and her flare-ups became largely a thing of the past. Alpha-She watched, smiled and wondered; who could say what part the little Omega's friendship had played in Pippa's recovery?

Clifford it seemed felt a special affinity with the newcomer.

"I know what it feels like," he told her one sunny day in June as they strolled around the foothills. "I was four years old too when I came here, and everyone knew the rules but me: things like not going through a door before the Alpha-Pair, and sitting down whilst you were given your dinner. It was scary and I'd never lived in before either, so sometimes I forgot the drill for going outside to have a pee. But you'll soon learn Pippa; don't let Destiny get you down. She is so strong and feisty and the pack needs that but she can be a bit off-putting too."

"Thanks, Clifford. I do like being here and more than anything want to belong to the Pack. Do you think I'll be allowed to stay?"

"I can't see the Alpha-Pair packing you off now Pipsqueak!"

Pippa stopped and turned to look at him. "Why do you call me that?" she asked a trifle crossly.

"Because you squeak and squeal whenever you hear Alpha-She coming – especially if she is carrying your dinner!"

"Cheek!" She nipped him playfully.

Clifford bucked then dipped low at the front, paws outstretched and chest to ground, haunches raised in the air in the ancient sign of the play bow.

Responding, Pippa jumped him then gave chase when he darted away. They spent an enjoyable few minutes in mock dominance and courting play, with Clifford nipping the back of her neck and nuzzling her ear whilst she pranced and danced and whipped around to present him with her rear, then shot back again. Panting and exhilarated they paused to get their breath.

"You can stay for me anyway," Clifford whispered. "You're a pretty little bitch, if a tad sassy!"

Pippa's mouth turned a deep shade of pink, but today at least, this had little to do with the pollen count.

Clifford whispers sweet nothings in Pippa's ear

Call of the Wild

6.

Fenella tells of how she found Tilly in time . . . and D'Arcy disappears

D'Arcy stood apart from the others as they strolled, or in the case of the youngsters played, on the lower slope of the fell. He stared out across the valley to the blue and mauve mountains beyond and felt the familiar rush of adrenalin tempered by a flutter of fear deep in his belly. Yet if he was ever going to go it had to be now. Despite being firmly in denial, he could no longer ignore the signs: with the passing of the Autumnal days Joey was becoming thinner and tired more easily. On more than one occasion he had caught Alpha-She weighing up Joey with sadness in her eyes. Yet he was eating well and a visit to the vet-man had revealed no obvious reason other than the march of Time. Lady

Moon was yet again rising to the full and only that morning Destiny had remarked upon the thickening and darkening of pelt running along his spine. The yearning was upon him too; an itching of feet and twitching of muscles that left him more torn apart than ever. As though picking up on his thoughts she appeared now at his side.

"You won't go and leave us now, will you D'Arcy?" she asked, her voice tight with anxiety.

"You've noticed too."

"Yes, Joey is growing tired." Destiny's mouth turned down at the corners. "How will we get through it?" she whispered.

"With the help of Alpha-She – and Ben."

"Yes, he will come to take him home." Ever aware of these things, Destiny spoke quietly and matter of factly. "But not yet."

"No."

"And you will be here for us too."

"None of us ever know 'when', Destiny."

"But you will be here?" she insisted.

D'Arcy failed to answer and looked out instead across the valley to the distant mist-shrouded mountains. So he was unaware of the deep scrutiny of his sister, and the spark of anger and despair within her eyes.

Now it transpired that one evening soon after this conversation someone suggested a story-fest and somehow Fenella had got herself chosen as Tale-teller. Somebody mentioned Tilly and the night she was lost, and when Fenella protested they were all there at the time so knew the ending, Pippa piped up to say she wasn't, and therefore didn't. Nan Tickle contributed one of her whiskers of wisdom by pointing out to the younger girls that Pack Story Telling was about keeping well-loved legends alive and as such, they could never be told too often. The trick to keeping them fresh, she added with a smile for her youngest charges, was to always tell them as though for the first time. Fenella nodded and agreed to tell Tilly's Tale. The nights were drawing in and recently had been frosted with white, and they all lay within the warmth of the Aga to listen. Destiny tensed and sat up, her eyes searching the twilit room, then as they rested upon her brother she relaxed and settled once more. D'Arcy looked away and appeared pre-occupied but at least he was there with them. Fenella cleared her throat, and managing to appear both proud and nervous at one and the same time, began to tell the story:

She started hesitantly, looking round at her audience to check they were listening. Their laid back ears and intent expressions — just discernible in the deepening twilight — gave her the confidence to carry on.

Fenella tells her First Story

It happened one evening in November when the leaves were stiff with cold and the ground white with frost . . . and we had just returned from a trip to the family business with Alpha-She. We had been away for several days, staying in our comfortable heated quarters and outside run during the day whilst Alpha-She was at the office, then sharing the house with her at night and having special supper treats for being good. We enjoyed the change, and there was lots of space to run, play and explore in the huge garden with the salty breeze and roar of the sea in the background. We were looking forward to being home again though, but it was a long ride back even in our special Jo-mobile car, and despite its safety cages and comfy mattresses it got hairy coming over the icy fell in the dark. There was a large moon though and by its light I could see the steep twisty road glistening and white. A couple of times we slid to one side of our cages and braced ourselves by digging in our feet (and I know people laugh at them, but my big feet came in handy here as I had extra grip!).

"Time for four-wheel drive, kids," Alpha-She called over her shoulder.

I don't know exactly what that means but the engine sound changed and we stopped skidding and climbed to the top of the mountain with ease.

We had been here in the house for about an hour and the bustle of unloading, fetching and settling had finally been done, when Alpha-She came into the kitchen with a worried look on her face. "Have any of you seen Tilly since we came back?" and when we all looked blank she demanded "Where's Tilly?" Now that we did understand. We all started scooting around the kitchen and hall looking for our little mate. There was no sign of her, and Alpha-She went from room to room calling her name (very loudly and in a voice that hurt my ears, because Tilly was deaf but could hear some high-pitched sounds) and looking under beds and behind chairs and cupboards and I – being the littlest one – wriggled under the sofa and the settle but still no Tilly. I was truly worried because being something of a Scallop (or something like that Alpha-She calls it) oh, thanks Destiny, yes that's it – an Escapologist – I knew exactly what it is like to be lost, scared and waiting to be rescued. Alpha-She was worried too, she kept saying about Tilly being seventeen years old and it was freezing hard outdoors. Eventually, she shrugged on a fleece, jammed a hat on her head and grabbed a torch from the porch. Instructing us to stay in the house and be good, and as Alpha-He had set off for the business hours earlier to take over from her, Alpha-She went off alone in search of Tilly.

Some time later we heard the door open and shut and expected to hear Alpha-She telling Tilly off for staying out late and loving her for being safe but there was a stony silence. "There's no sign of her anywhere," Alpha-She said miserably, wiping tears from her face and pacing up and down. I sat alone by the door, listening and puzzling because I sensed that Tilly was somewhere close yet beyond hearing Alpha-She's frantic calls and high pitched whistles. If she was so near the house why couldn't she hear? Then a light went on inside my head. Tilly was too poorly to come home and we had to find her fast. Like you Aunty Destiny, I sometimes sense these things. Alpha-She had stopped pacing and was watching me with a thoughtful expression.

"You know where she is, don't you Little One," she said quietly.

Striding to the door she yanked it open and cried "Go, all of you, go with Fenella and find Tilly!"

As one, we raced through the door into the compound and Alpha-She threw open the gate. We streamed through, running blind and not really sure what to do, but I listened with my inner ear as I asked for help and direction. I ducked low as a fierce shriek sounded above my head. A white shape glided before me and I knew it was a sign. "Help me *please*, Hushwing Ghost-Owl," I panted, "Help me find poor Tilly." Another shriek told me she had heard and also that I must hurry. I followed as she swooped low over the woodshed, turning her heart-shaped face to make sure I was following, then rose and disappeared above the frosted trees. The nearer I drew, the surer I became, and also the more aware of the urgency. My feet flew over icy ground and my breath rose in little white clouds and became trapped in frozen moonbeams. Alpha-She's voice rang in my ears as I ran.

"That's it Fenella, find Tilly!"

You were all left behind, hampered by freezing dark and lack of direction. As I reached the woodshed I knew Hushwing had brought me to be the right place, or rather to the old open-ended Nissan Hut alongside. I flew in, scattering a layer of dried leaves at least a tail's length deep and stood for a second, sniffing and listening for signs of Tilly. A beam of light flashed around the corner of the woodland run and a shadow darkened the moonlit entrance. Alpha-She watched in silence and I felt little daggers of her tension run over my skin as I ducked beneath an old garden bench and wriggled beneath. My nose touched something soft but horribly cold and it smelled of Tilly. My body shot out backwards as I dug in and pushed with my big front paws and I whipped round and gave three sharp barks of warning. Alpha-She immediately dropped onto her hands and knees in the loam, then lay full length to reach under the bench. She emerged clutching a tiny body. Her hands gently felt it all over, then taking off her ancient but still incredibly soft cashmere scarf, Alpha-She wrapped Tilly in it and carried her outside.

"Well done, Fenella," she breathed, "Tilly is unconscious but still alive! Let's get her indoors – and quick!"

By this time you had all gathered around to watch and whisper, and we trooped behind Alpha-She as she walked home at a smart pace with little Tilly held snugly to her breast.

"Thank you Hushwing Ghost-Owl," I murmured, knowing that she would be watching from somewhere unseen. A single high-pitched shriek told me she had heard and that my gratitude was appreciated.

We followed Alpha-She indoors in an unusually quiet and orderly fashion for us, because we sensed that Tilly was close to going over the Rainbow Bridge. Alpha-She wrapped her in warm blankets and made her a bed near the log fire. When Tilly eventually came round, Alpha-She fed her every couple of hours from a dropper with warmed milk, honey and a spot of brandy. The next day, as you know, she was taken to the vet hospital and we all fretted until Alpha-She returned and we could see that Tilly was still this side of Rainbow Bridge! Soon she was eating titibits of salmon and chicken and lapping her strengthening milk concoction, but was kept indoors. It was great to watch her from the doorway and hear her weak answering cry when we took it in turns to bark 'hello'.

The week that followed was a happy and very loving one for Tilly and the Alpha-Pair. They showered Tilly with care and affection and kept her snug and warm in their company by a constantly blazing log fire. But there was a sadness too, because deep inside they knew what we already sensed, that this was to be Tilly's last days with them and so each one was precious. They were determined to make this a happy time though with no sadness or regret, and to simply enjoy the time that was left. Then one cold but sunny Friday, exactly a week after Tilly had been found, she made it clear that she wanted to go outside. We could all see that Alpha-She was unsure and wavering, but Tilly cried out with a voice almost as strong as before her illness, demanding to be let out. Alpha-She looked worried as she released the catch on the cat flap and Tilly went through, but we were all relieved to see a smile on her face as she watched from the window as Tilly washed herself in the sunlight.

Tilly returned some time later and walked into the kitchen. She came to each of us in turn and touched us with her nose, and said "Thanks for having me in the Pack, guys." We all said things like "Honoured to have you little matey!", and "Great to see you up and about again," but we all knew that she was saying goodbye. She had been determined to go out in the sunlight, had done it, and was now making ready to go to Ellie and the other sisters and brothers she had outlived. Alpha-She looked so pleased and relieved to see back safely inside that our hearts hurt for what was to come. After settling Tilly in her bed on the chair by the fire, Alpha-She took us out for our run on the fell. We had been there only minutes when she stopped dead in the middle of a game of chase and listened intently.

"It's Tilly!" she cried, though we had heard nothing. "She needs me!" She began to run to the fell gate, calling over her shoulder sharply for us to follow.

Tilly on the Fell in Snow

We watched from the doorway, and saw Alpha-She on her knees by Tilly's chair. Tilly was in a deep sleep from which we knew she would not wake up. Alpha-She scooped her up in the blankets and told us to be good as she had to get Tilly to the vets. But Tilly wanted none of that. She had spent this day as she had most wanted, basking in fresh air and sunlight and in the loving company of Alpha-She and the Pack. Her eyes remained closed and she drifted peacefully over the Rainbow Bridge in her chosen way: held close in Alpha-She's arms. We were all sad, of course – but happy for her too, because Tilly had gone with so much love to join Ellie and the other brothers and sisters. Anyway, I'm sure she still hangs around us – I see her sometimes, peeping from under a bush as she stalks birds, or washing herself in the sunshine just as she did that last day – then she disappears like mist in sunlight.

Fenella's voice sounded quieter and held a slight tremor as she shared this last bit of her story. She looked round at the others, a troubled look in her dark oval eyes, then stared down at the floor with embarrassment.

"It's all right, Fenella, I've seen her too." It was Destiny who had spoken and in a kindly manner. "You are like me," she added, "able to see and hear what the others can not. Don't be frightened or embarrassed by it."

"Thank you, Destiny," Fenella said, looking pleased with this obvious show of support.

"That is one of the loveliest stories I've ever heard," Pippa said, looking dewy-eyed and emotional. "Thank you so much for telling it for me Fenella."

"Yes, that was well-told, and well done too, Little One," Joey added from where he lay relaxing on his huge bed. "Our Tilly was a little cracker and no mistake!"

"Yes, Destiny told me the story about Tilly being lost on Misty Mountain – it was real exciting – and Tilly was so brave and funny too!" Pippa chipped in.

"Yep, that was a fab tale!" Clifford enthused. "And Granddad Ben was right: Tickle proved to be the bravest brood bitch on the Planet!"

"It was nothing, really," Tickle said modestly, but turning pink with pleasure.

"And now we're stuck with that mad Marley-cat," Clifford said sulkily.

"I like stalking him actually," Pippa admitted, but touching her nose with her paw at the memory of his claws when she got too close. "But why did the Alpha-Pair let him come and live here? I mean, after Tilly, well it sounds like she left huge paw-prints to fill!" she added.

"His elderly mistress got sick and died and nobody else would have him," Flossie supplied. "There was talk I believe of – *The RSPCA!*" she added in hushed tones.

"What's that – a sort of cat Boot Camp?" Pippa asked frowning and Flossie nodded.

"Best place for him if you ask me!" Clifford said, blinking and looking the other way as though he had not spoken.

"He's a handsome cat though," Tickle broke in, "with that soft apricot and his whites really sparkle. He has lovely colouring – much like my own really," she added, raising secretive smiles from the others.

"He can shin up a tree like a squirrel – intelligent too. Pity he's so bolshi, but he has balls, you have to admit," Destiny commented, "Suppose he has to have really; I doubt he'd even seen a dog before let alone had to live with seven!"

"I suppose we have no choice but to put up with him," Flossie said glumly.

Nobody noticed Marley skulking outside the kitchen door or saw him quietly turn and leave. And if he was hurting, well he sure as hell wasn't going to let that Setter rabble know it.

"Whatever, how clever of you Fenella, to have found our dear Tilly," Nan Tickle said, skilfully changing the thorny subject. "She would have died out there alone in the freezing cold," she added giving Fenella's paw a lick of approval.

"Instead she had a love-filled week with us and the Alpha-Pair – so we mustn't be sad, we must celebrate her long and happy life," Clifford contributed, then rolled his large liquid eyes to the ceiling and stuck out that left ear in embarrassment at having offered this unusual-for-him piece of wisdom.

"Good lad, Clifford," Joey spoke up, "and we must all remember that wise advice in times to come."

Clifford sat up very straight and looked delighted at this praise, but Destiny was scrutinizing Joey with a worried look on her face.

"Is something wrong?" Pippa asked, but Destiny shook her head and said 'sorry I was somewhere else' and because she frequently was, the Pack thought nothing of it. Nevertheless, they all looked round at one another as though something or someone was missing.

"Where's D'Arcy?" somebody asked.

Into the Wilderness . . .

7.

A long way from home

He wanted to return already, even before stepping off the family land. Sneaking out whilst everyone was avidly listening to Fenella's story had been easy, and opening the back door by twisting the handle was no problem at all because he had chosen his time well: before nightfall, because then all the doors would be locked until the following morning; leaving instead as twilight melted the outline of tree and boulder and blended them with a Setter who did not wish to be seen. Carrying on alone into the unknown however was something very different. He had set off at a gallop, expecting at any moment to be called back. Then, as his absence had apparently gone unnoticed, his pace slowed to a steady lope that took him beneath the towering pine and fir trees that guarded their home. Their upturned branches reached into the night and allowed early moonbeams to filter through and pattern the floor of the woodland. It took him past the homestead's sentinel pines and on through the beech wood to shuffle through drifts of dried leaves torn from their precarious hold by a recent and chill north-westerly. Then on through the birch copse, the bare spindly arms purple-black and scratching against a mauve and greenish light, the last of the dying day.

The trees were becoming smaller and thinner as the ground rose to the foothills and became more exposed. He followed the deer track up onto the open fell and the loping stride slowed to a walk, not from fatigue but reluctance to leave this, his home. It faltered and he almost turned and ran back when the faint sound of voices calling his name reached him on the evening breeze. He climbed a large boulder and looked down the way he had come and his heart lurched and courage waned when he spotted the intermittent flashes of torchlight through the trees. The pain in his heart made him gasp and heave, but the moonbeams that silvered his coat strengthened the old familiar urge and he turned and fled. Once clear of the searchers he slowed to a thoughtful and questioning walk.

Upon reaching the boundary fence that walk slowed to a halt. D'Arcy stood looking at it, head lowered and tail tucked between legs. The insecure pup in his psyche arose and wailed: *I don't want to do this. I don't want to leave my home, my pack and most of all, I don't want to leave my beloved Alpha-She!* But that other self, the mature and confident one with the black eye flash and dark ridge along his back slid alongside and urged him on. *You have been chosen for this. You must see it through – for Grey Pelt and the good of the pack. Go on, jump! Freedom is only a stride away!* it whispered in his ear. I could stay the night in the old den built for the human-child nearly two decades ago, he thought. When passing it he had noticed that the roof of woven branches had sunk but was still in place and the opening was high enough for a Setter in need of shelter to creep through. He would stay there till morning light, he decided, and then make his decision. If you do that, the wolf within whispered, you will never leave; as the sun comes up you will turn for home. D'Arcy chose to ignore it. He started visibly as an ear-splitting screech sounded overhead to shatter the silence. The white owl swung low and screeched a second time, turning a heart-shaped face to stare at him with huge yellow eyes. *Go now youngster, go! The time has come to honour your lineage.*

The words came through her eerie screeches to speak clearly to D'Arcy. He shuddered as a couple of lines from one of Destiny's songs spontaneously ran through his head:

> *When Hushwing flies and bats are at play,*
> *Grey Pelt is never far away!*

Struck motionless by indecision he watched Hushwing swoop then rise into the darkening sky, her screech tailing off into the night. As he faltered a heavy and pregnant silence blanketed the darkening fell, then as he stiffened and waited for what he knew would come next, a thin high wail drifted down from the summit.

Grey Pelt!

Half-enthralled, half-afraid he listened as the wail bellied out, rising and falling in a crescendo of wolf-song to haunt the soul. The ridge along his back bristled and his muscles bulged and begged for action. On legs magically elongated he loped forward, paused, crouched and sprang. In one clear leap he was over the boundary wall and running in answer to the call.

As the night wore on, D'Arcy neither heard nor saw anything more of Grey Pelt and he began to suspect a conspiracy to get him over that wall. At first he had run on adrenalin and with mind clouded by euphoria – hoping perhaps to see a silhouette darkening the moon at the summit of the mountain. But as he cleared the sycamore wood and headed across farmland dotted with cattle and sheep, the fells that marched across the horizon loomed bare and empty. He had slowed to a trot and every hundred paces or so, paused to turn and look back in the direction of home. Already homesick, he faltered. If he was going to turn back it had to be now. The full moon, unhampered by cloud, sent stark brittle light streaming across field and woodland, striking the silver bark of birch and rowan, silvering gorse and bracken and exposing him to every sort of danger. However, shadows were deepened by contrast, and wherever he could he skulked in the lea of wall or hedge and determined to go on. To return now, tail between legs, would be shameful and he had no stomach for facing Joey with failure. Soon he left behind the lowland fields and began to climb the foothills. On he pressed, unaware of the moving shadow that shrank into the deepest shade of the wall whenever he paused and turned his head.

The pull on his thigh muscles increased and the bitter cold penetrated his coat. Depressed and weary he paused at the edge of the hanging moor and stared in dismay at a vast expanse of bracken and wind-bleached grass that offered no cover to a fugitive. For that is how he now felt: a homeless rover who had abandoned his home and pack in a secretive and shameful way. His nerve failing, he started and veered sideways then realised the beast barring his way was merely an oddly-shaped boulder. Heart thumping he asked himself for the hundredth time what he was doing here, and why.

You are here on a mission that only the bold and those who carry the mark may undertake!

D'Arcy ducked his head as a splayed shadow darkened the ground at his feet, then daring to raise it he stared up at the midnight sky. The ghostly white shape of Hushwing, feathers splayed and awesome, hovered on the moonlight.

"Hushwing!"

Follow me, and I shall keep you company on your way.

With this she veered round and with slow and measured beat of her wings set out across the moonlit moor. Reluctantly, but feeling he had no choice, D'Arcy followed.

Hushwing turned and circled overhead, warning him to take extra care as they approached the dry wall boundary of a remote hill farm. Hushwing glided to and fro and from side to side, guiding him along sheep tracks and avoiding becks and gullies half-hidden by winter-scorched bracken. Then there it was, visible as they topped a rise and looked down into the hollow, a square stone-walled building rising in lonely defiance, the pewter of moon-washed roof slates in stark contrast to the black shiny glass of the windows. Except for one that is, on the ground floor where a yellow light glowed and warned of humans within. Several outbuildings including a barn surrounded the farmhouse. Hushwing, her customary shriek muted, made a whirring sound of caution and glided down into the depression, turning her heart-shaped face to check if D'Arcy was following.

He sensed rather than heard the threat of low growls seconds before the cacophony of barking broke loose. The door to the barn shuddered with the impact of unseen paws being slammed against it with force.

"Run!" Hushwing shrieked. "Run, but stay low!"

So saying she wheeled and hovered, white wings splayed against midnight sky and feathers silvered by moonlight. A fearsome screech brought up D'Arcy's hackles and set the farm dogs clamouring even more frantically for release.

The curtains at the lighted window were not drawn (little point, the occupants must have thought, living in this uninhabited wilderness) and the figure of a man appeared dark against the light at his back.

Almost immediately the door was thrown back and he stood framed in the opening, shotgun in hand.

"What's up wi' the dogs?" a female voice called from within.

"Dunno. This pesky owl set 'em off I reckon, but I'll let 'em out just in case."

In five strides he was at the barn door. As he flung it open three sheepdogs shot out and a volley of barks ricocheted round the mountains. Falling over themselves in their eagerness to challenge the stranger, they tore across the farmyard and through the open gate. D'Arcy did indeed run for his life. Belly almost touching the ground he swerved round boulders and leapt over streams and only once chanced a look over his shoulder. The farm dogs were gaining; they were rested whereas he had been on the run for most of the night and was now tiring.

"It's a stray dog – must sense lambing will be early this year!"

D'Arcy's heart almost stopped as the farmer's voice travelled across the high moor. He knew from Alpha-She what happened to dogs that were suspected of worrying sheep; she was always warning the pack to stay on their own land. The explosion from the gun failed to register, so intent was he on escape. He started and half turned at the deafening noise but hardly checked his pace. The first he knew of it was the shock of pain as something hit his left haunch. He faltered then kept on running but eventually the stabbing of red hot needles brought him down. The pursuing dogs, seeing his plight, bayed with excitement and increased their pace. He struggled upright. Their blood was up and they were out of control. If he didn't at least try to move on he would soon be seriously bitten before being shot by the irate farmer. His haunch burned and felt hot and sticky. Unable to do more than limp forward, dragging his injured hind leg, he heard the panting of his pursuers close behind and knew they were almost upon him. Whirling round, he stopped and faced them, determined at least to go down fighting.

Then came help from an unexpected quarter.

"Crawl away, find somewhere to hide!" Hushwing hissed from behind his left ear. Swooshing in like an avenging angel, feet and talons outspread and ready to grasp her prey, Hushwing uttered a scream that made the hills shudder and D'Arcy's ears ring. It also stopped the pursuers in their tracks so that the last two collided into their leader. Hushwing hovered just above and in front of them, effectively shielding D'Arcy whilst he made his slow and tortuous escape. Hushwing loosed a volley of eerie shrieks and dived to earth. A yelp of pain and shock, followed by another and yet another, made D'Arcy pause to look. The sheepdogs, clawed, bloodied and abashed had turned tail and were racing back the way they had come. The angry shouts and whistles of the farmer rounding up his dogs, followed by the slam of a door, allayed any fears of the gun. With a shriek of triumph Hushwing wheeled, hovered and perched on the overhanging branch of wind-stunted rowan.

"I reckon you scared *him* to death too," D'Arcy panted, rising painfully to his feet. "Thank you, Hushwing, you saved my life," he added humbly.

"This time; but there is much danger ahead," she counseled in her high wispy voice. "And now you must move on and find a safe place for the night."

With these words Hushwing flapped her great wings and rose into the night where she hovered, a ghostly white form against a midnight sky. A wave of panic and dismay swept over D'Arcy so that he called out piteously "Don't leave me alone Hushwing, *please!*"

"That is part of the test, D'Arcy."

"I've been shot, and I have no food or shelter!"

"You will survive – if you believe!"

"Believe what?" D'Arcy cried, his voice high with panic.

"In your unseen helpers. And I shall never be far away."

The great wings swept forward and down to give lift, and soon she was an eerie white speck fast disappearing into the night. One spine-chilling shriek wavered across the ether to haunt him, then Hushwing was gone.

The silence that followed the last echo of that cry filled D'Arcy with desolation. Alone for the very first time in his life, he crept miserably away. Pain, weariness and distress deadened his faculties but instinct directed him away from the site of possible and immediate danger. He limped along, flank afire, and consumed by hunger and thirst. At least this moor was riddled with running becks at which he was able to drink and quench the fire within. The constant moorland music of water trickling and gurgling over stone was a sound that D'Arcy found strangely comforting. It made him feel a little less alone in the flat, treeless wilderness in which he now found himself. He longed to lie down in one of the becks and let the icy water cool his inflamed leg, but instinct warned him not to do so. The night was growing colder by the minute, and earth and branch sparkled with a dusting of frost. He had no food to create energy for warmth. If his core temperature dropped he risked death from hypothermia.

A frosty night ahead

Miss Tickle: Pack Nanny and Guardian

8.

The Pack bereft . . . and Tickle tells a cheering tale

Those first days following D'Arcy's disappearance were amongst the worst in the Pack's history. Apart from grief upon the passing of past members nothing had touched them so deeply or left them so raw. It could even be said that those events, though devastating, were understandable as the natural passing and changing of Life-force, and therefore easier to bear than this dreadful unknowing.

"Is Uncle D'Arcy out there somewhere and hurting?" Little Fenella worried, scratching an ear and looking vulnerable and confused.

"He mustn't be able to come back to us, or he would be here now." It was Flossie who had spoken with devastating logic, and like her sister, she looked haunted and distressed.

"That's right, he would never leave and stay away of his own free will," Pippa added, her black mask crinkled in misery.

"He's a big brave lad and strong with it, so I'm sure he will be all right," Nanny Tickle reassured her young charges.

She looked to Destiny for back-up but she seemed far away in a world of her own. This was nothing new. She had taken to going off alone for hours at a time, searching for her missing brother. At first the Alpha-Pair remonstrated with her on her return, but then realised it did not prevent her going and only added to the stress.

"Isn't that right, Destiny?" Tickle demanded, stomping the floor with a front paw to command attention.

"What's that? Oh yes, yes of course he will," Destiny murmured before walking away and sitting in a corner alone.

"She's worried for her brother," Joey excused her whilst nodding sagely, "Remember they've never been separated before."

"Yes, of course, it must be awful for her," Tickle conceded, but her eyes narrowed slightly as she looked across at Destiny.

Always quick to catch on, Clifford moved closer. "Do you think she knows something Tickle?"

"If she did, I'm sure she would tell us," Tickle said firmly, moving away to avoid further questions.

Despite the depth of their misery, the worst part of it all was being witness to Alpha-She's grief. She constantly went outside, calling his name with tears in her eyes then when there was no response, returning indoors and hurrying away from them so that they would not have to witness her grief. But they heard it, the heart-breaking sobbing and murmured words of "Oh, D'Arcy, where are you? Please, please come back to me!" Then she would return to the kitchen and make a pot of tea and sit amongst them, reassuring them with forced cheer and false words, telling them D'Arcy had just gone off on an adventure and would be back any time now, but despite all her well-meant subterfuge, they sensed she did not believe it. But it helped, to feel the warm cloak of her love around them, and to know that she shared their misery and despair. The weather had turned wintry, yet several times a day Apha-She kitted herself up in warm outdoor clothes and donned her fell boots to tramp the fields and hills calling D'Arcy by name. At night she went out with a light strapped to her head and stick in hand, climbed the slippery slopes of the fell in search of her beloved boy. The worse time had been that first night when the Alpha-Pair, once they realised D'Arcy was missing, had searched throughout the night and returned at dawn weary, defeated – and without D'Arcy.

Despite words of denial to Clifford, Tickle chose her time and confronted Destiny when she was alone.

"If you know something, Destiny, you have to speak to the Pack," she said sternly, eyeballing the younger bitch to emphasise her status as the Pack Matriarch and Guardian.

"Like what?" Destiny retorted, her voice brittle and manner defensive.

"Like where D'Arcy is!" Tickle shot back.

"How should I know, he went without a word to me."

"You two were so close, and you so fey, you knew something was going on without being told!"

"I sensed it was to do with You-know-who, and that D'Arcy is carrying something within him that has to be resolved, but that's all I know."

"Come now Destiny, we both knew he was planning to go. He spoke to me about it from time to time, so I'm damned sure he confided in you, his beloved sister!" Tickle said roundly.

"Don't pull the guilt one on me Tickle! I love him too, you know."

"I know, dear, I know," Tickle relented, her gaze softening and she blinked twice to show there was no ill feeling. "But we both know what this is about, and we have to reassure the pack that he hasn't just run away, been stolen or fallen in the lake and drowned!"

"I don't know any more than you do Tickle," Destiny persisted stubbornly.

"I'll have a word after supper if you like, but there's not much I can say."

"Is everything all right here girls?"

They both whirled round to find Joey eyeing them suspiciously and with an expression of disapproval. "We've enough upset in the Pack at present, without the Elders falling out," he said sternly.

"No fall out Joe," Tickle said with one of her winning smiles. "Destiny and I were just having a discussion."

"Oh yes?" Joey gave her a skeptical look and raised one eyebrow.

"Yes, about how best to move the Pack forward," Tickle retorted unabashed. "And Destiny here came up with the excellent idea of talking to the Pack, the younger members especially, after supper to let them know D'Arcy has left for a reason."

"And what might that be?"

"Oh, I'm sure you have an idea, Joey," Tickle said raising her eyebrows to give him a quizzical look. Joey was quiet for a moment before speaking again.

"It seems you may know something you shouldn't too, Tickle."

"Maybe," she said with a sad little smile and eyes shadowed by fleeting sorrow. Destiny looked away, aware of the crackle of emotion between them. Joey frowned and almost imperceptibly shook his head; Tickle quickly smiled again.

"Very well, do what you can to make them feel better Destiny," Joey ruled.

Destiny nodded and Tickle had to be satisfied with that.

Destiny was true to her word. After they had nibbled half-heartedly at their supper and lapped up some if not all of their milk, and Alpha-She had gone outside to keep her usual vigil, Destiny stood before them.

"I want to speak to you about D'Arcy," she began, "He is my brother, and I would give one of my legs willingly to have him here with me tonight, and I know all of you feel the same. But there is something you should know. D'Arcy would not approve of me telling you this, but Nanny Tickle feels you have suffered much already and need to be reassured."

"By what, Destiny? Are you able to tell us he is alive and well?" Pippa said, leaning forward in her eagerness to hear.

"Wait." Destiny held up a paw to stem any further questions. "I can only say that he has not run away, or been abducted or acted without thought for us all."

"Then where is he – and why isn't he here with us?" Flossie demanded, chewing her lip in frustration.

"He has been sent on a mission of great importance."

"What can be more important than being here with us?" Clifford demanded, his usually sparkling dark eyes now lack-lustre and brimming with sadness.

"The future of the Pack – all packs, whether wild or domestic," Destiny said shortly.

"But what sort of mission?"

"He is like Great Aunt Fenella, he carries the mark – and the burden," little Fenella spoke up quietly, and a hush fell over the pack.

"What's that?" Clifford said frowning.

"I don't properly understand," Fenella said in little more than a whisper, her eyes vague and seeming to be looking elsewhere at a world that lay beyond them in the manner they were more used to seeing in Destiny. "But it is to do with the one of whom we should not speak."

"You mean Grey . . ."

"Don't utter his name!" Destiny broke in fiercely. "You should know the rule by now Pippa!"

"Sorry, Destiny." Pippa looked abashed and lowered her head onto her paws in submission.

"But you believe D'Arcy to be on this Quest, whatever it may be, and that he will return one day fit and well?" Nanny Tickle prompted, turning to Destiny.

"Yes, yes I feel sure he will," Despite the firmness of her voice Destiny dropped her gaze to the floor.

"There now, we all feel better don't we?" Tickle said perhaps a little too brightly. "We have to have faith that the Great-Mother-in-the-Sky will look after him and bring him home to us safe and sound," she added, turning to look sternly at each member in turn until they nodded in agreement.

"There now, and just to celebrate that feeling, I shall tell you all a story!"

So rare was this event that the pack members gathered round and were able for a short time at least to put aside their abject misery and longing, and to pretend they could not hear the anguish in Alpha-She's voice as she patrolled the grounds calling to her boy.

Now this, Tickle began settling down before the Aga, is a story about Fenella the Second when she was a pup, passed down by Tawny, the collie-retriever and little Becky the border collie, both of whom had been rescued by the Alpha-Pair. Fenella the Second was the big dark bolshi one of the pair, her sister of course being Flossie the Second who was whiter in coat and gentler by nature."

"Well, at least you got the white coat, Flossie!" Clifford quipped, chuckling behind his paw.

"Cheek! I'm gentle too," Flossie shot back, pretending to look hurt but trying not to grin.

"Oh yeah? Is that why you are always treading on Alpha-She's toes or butting Alpha-He on the head?"

"I can't help getting excited," Flossie said in injured tones. "It's just part of my extra loving nature."

"I know that one," Clifford said nodding. "When I'm happy I have fireworks going off inside me, *bing-bang-bang*, and stars shooting all over the place!"

"Yes, we know Clifford," the others chorused.

"But not now, I'm not happy now," he murmured, his huge dark eyes swimming with sadness.

"No," Destiny said flatly, and they all fell silent.

The silence, however, was broken by the tapping of Nanny Tickle's forepaw on the floor. "Right, are we all ready now to hear this tale or am I going to bed?" she reproved them, but nobody took offence because they knew she was trying to pull them back again, out of the morass of grief that was D'Arcy.

"Sorry Nan Tickle, yes do please go ahead," Joey said with his own Top Dog grave dignity.

"Okie-diddle, it goes like this," Tickle said brightly, valiantly resuming the tale in her formal story-telling voice complete with the 'character voices' that she knew the pack found so entertaining:

The pups Fenella and Flossie the Second were about twelve months old when it happened. Alpha-She had let them out to toilet and Fenella had gone AWOL over the dry stone wall (as she would). Flossie being the smaller one couldn't quite make it to the top so was left behind. She fretted and worried and paced up and down and heaved a sigh of relief when Fenella appeared, hot and panting from running all the way home. "Quick!" she gasped, "You must go get Alpha-She and get her to come and look for me."

"Why? You're already here!" Flossie said looking confused.

"There's a ewe fallen down the ravine. Two silly walkers let their dog chase it off the edge. If she thinks I'm missing she'll come looking and then we can get her to help. Now stop asking questions and go get Alpha-She!" Fenella barked. "I'll go back down to the river – you must get her to follow you there. Now go!"

So Flossie ran back to the door and barked to warn Alpha-She that something was amiss.

"What is it, Flossie?" Alpha-She cried on seeing her little favourite looking so distressed. "Where's Fenella? Oh no, has she gone missing again!"

Flossie barked and pumped her paw to tell her she had it right and ran for the gate with Alpha-She following close behind. They set off down the lane with Flossie leading the way.

"So there you are!" Alpha-She exclaimed as they reached the river and saw Fenella on the bank. Before Alpha could deliver a ticking-off and order her home again, Fenella ran a few paces along the riverside path then turned to see if they were following.

"Come, Fenella!" Alpha-She commanded, frowning in annoyance. "That's enough!"

Fenella ran further along the path and paused again. Flossie ran forward to join her and they both stood and barked at Alpha-She.

"What is it? What's wrong – you're obviously trying to tell me something!"

Alpha-She exclaimed, running fingers through her hair in frustration before setting off in pursuit. Once sure that Alpha-She was following, Fenella led them along the track to the bridge that spanned the river where it coursed through a sheer chasm and widened out to form a deep and rocky pool.

A man and a woman dressed in rambling gear and holding an excited terrier on a leash were standing near the edge of the ravine.

"Oh, thank goodness someone has come!" the woman cried, then bent to remonstrate ineffectively with the terrier that was barking frantically and dancing about at the end of the leash.

"Why, what's wrong?" Alpha-She asked, frowning at her futile efforts.

"Jack here chased a sheep and it fell over the edge," the man volunteered shamefacedly.

"And it's still alive?" Alpha-She said sounding skeptical.

"Oh yes, but it can't get up!"

"I'm not surprised! So why let your dog off-lead if he chases sheep?" Alpha-She demanded crossly, walking to the edge to peer over.

"We didn't think," the man said lamely.

"Obviously." Alpha-She leant over the edge and peered down at the shaggy Herdwick ewe that was lying half in, half out of the water with one leg bent at a suspicious angle. "Poor thing. It's a miracle it's still alive. That's a thirty-foot drop onto the rocks," she said grimly. "I'll run back and telephone the farmer to come," she said moving back to the path. "Wait here you two," she ordered Flossie and Fenella. "I can go faster on my own."

She ran back along the path and was soon out of sight.

She returned five minutes or so later, chest heaving, face red from exertion and with a coiled rope slung over one shoulder.

"There's no-one answering," she panted. "We'll have to manage ourselves."

She ran to the edge and turned to look inquiringly at the couple.

"Oh, I *couldn't*," the woman simpered, stepping back a pace or two. "I would go dizzy even looking down there; I don't like heights."

"I daresay that ewe didn't either when your dog chased it off the edge!" Alpha-She said roundly, "And what about you?" she said addressing the man.

"I'll stand at the edge if you want and help pull you up again," he offered half-heartedly.

"Thanks!" Alpha-She gave him a withering look and Fenella whispered in her sister's ear, "What a wimp!" Alpha-She shook her head as though to say 'what's the use' and hitched the coil of rope further onto her shoulder and began to pick her way down the face of jagged rocks. Flossie ran to the edge and started barking in agitation but Fenella bade her be quiet. "You'll distract her Floss. Our Alpha is a feisty bitch – she'll be all right!"

Gentle Flossie nodded, and with Fenella at one side, and the man stationed at the other, watched anxiously as Alpha-She made the perilous descent.

They peered over the edge as Alpha-She reached the ewe and made a valiant attempt to get its hindquarters out of the water and force it onto its feet. Nothing she did could persuade it to rise, and she shouted up to the ring of faces rimming the edge: "I think its leg's broken, it's probably done for, poor thing." However, Alpha-She was not one for giving up on an animal in distress and she tugged and pushed and pulled until she somehow managed to get it clear of the river and onto a flat rock. The sodden fleece weighed a ton and beads of sweat dropped from her brow and she panted painfully with the effort. Somehow she got the rope behind its forelegs, round its middle and tied in a knot on its back.

"Right, now we need to haul you up!" she said grimly.

She began the return climb, unraveling the rope on the way and picking her route over boulders scoured into dish-shaped hollows, and rocks sculpted over the centuries into jagged teeth during times of spate when the level rose dramatically and the white-water gushed, tumbled and spumed its way down from the mountains. Aware of the danger, Flossie could not help a whimper of fear escaping and Fenella pressed against her flank to reassure her sister. About two thirds of the way up, Alpha-She paused and clinging onto a jutting rock with her left hand, prepared to throw the end of the rope to the watching man.

"Catch this and hold on to it," she shouted.

He nodded and missed the rope. It snaked back down the rock face and Alpha-She swayed dangerously whilst trying to retrieve it. The next attempt followed a similar pattern and Alpha-She shook her head in despair.

"For heaven's sake, grab it!"

At the third try he managed to catch it.

"When I tell you to, start to pull us up – but slowly!" she warned, then climbed down again to a by now very distressed ewe, eyes rolling back in its head and legs feebly scrambling for a hold.

"Take up the slack," she shouted.

As the rope tightened Alpha-She stepped gingerly into the water and balanced precariously on the mossed and slippery rocks beneath the surface. Grabbing handfuls of fleece she pushed and shoved to get the animal moving.

"Pull for heaven's sake – *pull!*" she urged the man who was peering over the edge instead of straining on the rope.

"Hold it there!" she instructed as the rope became taught, moving up behind the ewe so that its rear was resting on her right shoulder. "Pull us up, *now!*" Inch by painful inch the sheep began the steep ascent. Alpha-She strained and pushed with all her strength, strands of sodden and smelly wool impeding her sight and progress. The weight of the ewe and its saturated fleece was crippling, but at last they were poised within a foot or so from the top.

However, that last stretch was the steepest, with little or no hand and footholds available. "You'll have to help me!" she gasped, struggling to keep the animal stable and stop it from sliding back down and herself along with it. The sheep grunted and squirmed so that Alpha-She felt her shoulder must break beneath the weight.

"What was that?" The feckless man cupped his ear with one hand and the rope jerked and dropped as he struggled to hear above the barking terrier.

"Tie up that flaming dog, pass the rope to your missus, then get yourself down here to help me," Alpha-She yelled, now pushed way beyond politeness.

The man stared down at her helplessly, fear plain to see in his face. As his concentration slackened off, so did the rope and Alpha-She found herself sliding backwards, and scrambling for a foothold on the slippery rock face with the terrified ewe on top of her. "Get your arse down here and help me push – like *now!*" she yelled, her voice muffled by the wet fleece draped around her head and shoulders, but nevertheless managing the tones of one who was not to be ignored.

Fear of Alpha-She's fury overcame both dread of the climb and the man's reluctance to harangue his wife into tethering the yapping dog to a tree by its leash, and turn her hands to the rope which she reluctantly grabbed and hauled back on with all her weight. Turning a deaf ear to her grumbling, her man scrambled down to Alpha-She. He looked down at the river coursing too far below for comfort, and the ominous rocks that awaited any unwary move and began to tremble. Sweat beaded a face that had turned suddenly pale – and he froze.

"Get your shoulder behind it man – and push!" Alpha-She instructed, exasperated by his dithering and wet behaviour.

"Shove! Like *now*!" she roared in such a fierce voice that he automatically obeyed. One almighty heave later the ewe was propelled forward and up, to sprawl inelegantly upon safe ground.

It lay there for some time, eyes closed and flanks heaving. Alpha-She looked on anxiously while Flossie and Fenella sniffed with unbridled curiosity; it was the closest they had ever been to sheep.

"Come on, get up," Alpha-She cried, tugging at the sodden fleece to try and encourage the animal to rise. "It's going to peg out on us after all that effort!" she lamented, animosity for the couple who caused it forgotten now that the crisis was over.

"I feel really bad," the woman murmured, untying the culprit's lead to avoid looking Alpha-She in the face. "You're a bad lad, Jack!" she remonstrated with the now subdued terrier.

"So do I," the man admitted, still pale and panting from his exertions.

"It's not the dog's fault! But you did what you could in the end," Alpha-She added generously. "I'll go now and telephone the farmer to let him know to collect it," she said sadly, looking down at the still immobile victim.

As though having heard, it suddenly struggled upright and shot off in a flurry of wet fleece. Turning to give them all an indignant look, it squatted, had a pee and scooted off down the path to join its companions.

"What happened to the broken leg?" Alpha-She exclaimed, baffled but delighted as she watched its disappearing rump.

"It was playing possum!" the woman said, smiling shyly at Alpha-She.

"I reckon you're right! Well, I'm off now to get washed and changed," Alpha-She said, indicating her muddied and dripping clothes. "I smell like that ewe!"

"Thank you so much – and we're sorry we caused you so much trouble," the woman said in a rush.

"Glad it turned out okay. Just keep that pesky dog on a lead in future!" Alpha-She warned, and set off for home followed proudly by Flossie and Fenella.

That night Flossie and Fenella lay in their baskets and related the story for Tawny and Becky who made disparaging comments about the two walkers and their dog, and hugely enjoyed the embellished details provided by Fenella.

"Just one thing, sis," Flossie said as they all settled to for the night.

"What's that?" Fenella said sleepily.

"That ewe looked to be dying; what suddenly brought it to life and made it jump up like that?

"I nipped its bum!" Fenella explained, with a mischievous grin and characteristic wink that said it all.

Tickle finished her tale, and sat back with an expression of pure pleasure to listen to the giggles and comments of a pack who had for a while at least, forgotten their distress.

As they settled down on their beds ready for sleep, she dared to whisper in Joey's ear.

"Are you all right Joey?"

"Perfectly, why?"

"You seem more tired lately than usual that's all, and you're not eating much."

"I eat enough for my needs Tickle. I'm not so active these days. Besides, I've put on enough weight to live off my fat for a month!"

"Of course you have, Joey. Goodnight, dear boy."

"Goodnight, Tickle, and well done, you made them forget for a while."

Tickle lay down on her bed next to his and rested her head on his chest for mutual comfort. Always careful of Joey's pride, she had refrained from observing that despite putting on weight, building muscle and looking big and strong throughout the summer months, he now appeared thinner and a trifle frail. She shivered as though a cold wind had passed over them all.

Where are you D'Arcy? The Pack needs you!!"

Tickle's last thought as she drifted into uneasy sleep.

A cold and frosty morning

9.

Winter comes to the Fells
. . . and D'Arcy is in dire need

D'Arcy awoke shivering and moved stiffly to the entrance of his make-shift hideaway. He pushed aside the tracery of frosted branches that framed the opening and gazed out on a landscape transformed overnight into a Winterland of snow and ice. The mountain that stalked the horizon, and which he knew he would have to traverse, was covered in white and he knew himself to be in grave danger. With an untended wound that would likely fester, and no food in his belly, he could not hope to survive such a journey. Despite the intense cold his haunch burned and he whimpered with pain at each movement. He had been so stupid, he lamented; prior to leaving he had told no-one of his intended direction, (much less his destination as he did not know it) and the snow would have deadened his scent anyway so there was no chance of him being found – at least not in time. That thought chilled far more than any snow or ice. He had spared no thought for food and his basic needs for survival, and now he would pay with his life.

Cold, pain and hunger pangs gnawed at his body and darkened his mind, undermining courage and resolve. Pangs of homesickness assailed him too, and a heartfelt yearning to be enfolded in Alpha-She's embrace. His love for her became a pain that constricted his chest and left him gasping for breath. So intense were these feelings that had it been possible then he would have turned for home, but in his weakened state he would never make it. Then his spine stiffened and his head came up. If he was to perish out here alone in the wilderness, then at least he would do so with honour. She would not then be ashamed of me, he thought, if eventually my body is found they will all know I was pushing onward against impossible odds, rather than attempting to crawl home without even trying. It seemed then that an image of Grandsire Ben flashed into his mind, and he may have imagined it but it seemed he heard him say "Good lad, D'Arcy!" and the thought or whatever it was gave him heart. That, and the scent that was beginning to twitch at his nostrils. Curiosity and hunger drove him outside.

For the first time since being hounded by those murderous dogs, a spurt of hope flared in his breast. The scent of warm blood and flesh drove all thought from his mind. Not his chosen or usual diet but needs must, and it was received with gratitude. Only when he had eased his pangs and the small bones had been crunched along with the meagre amount of meat and the whole devoured, did he pause to wonder. Who could have left two small birds and a rat outside on the snow? He looked around and a spasm of shock shafted through him. *There are no footprints in the snow.* This realization filled him with fear of phantoms and things beyond this world, until certain words were repeated in his mind.

I shall never be far away.

Hushwing! Hushwing Ghost-Owl had dropped them for him to help him survive and continue his journey.

"Thank you, Hushwing," he murmured, his heart filled with gratitude.

The trickle of a beck made him realise he was thirsty and also that he needed to clean his mouth of the residual fur and feathers that were making him cough, retch and spit onto the snow. Following the sound he limped forward, spotting the pristine snow with droplets of his blood. With a couple of blows from his forepaw, he broke the skin of ice and drank greedily of the sweet water that tasted of moss and heather. Much restored, he crawled back into his hide and systematically began to lick his wound clean of blood and mucous to reduce the chance of it festering. Emerging once more he gazed at the mountain before him and relinquished any idea of a noble death. It was essential to keep moving, and whilst he had no idea where to, he set off at a slow and painful pace in response to the inward promptings. So intent was he on his goal that he failed to notice a stirring within the shadows, or the pair of eyes that from a distance watched his every move.

M. Just Joey: Show Champion and Beloved Top Dog

10.

Joey hears the call

As the days sped by, Tickle's unspoken fears proved justified. Joey became weaker and ever more frail, and at last the day came when he lay securely within Alpha-She's arms, closed his eyes for the last time and went peacefully home to his father. "Look after him, Ben," Alpha-She whispered through her tears.

These were dark days indeed for the Pack. The Alpha-Pair laid Joey to rest in the family's Setter Grotto and piled it high with flowers and blossom. Despite unselfish efforts to hide their grief it clung to them in greyish wisps, tangling with the pain of the Pack until a cobweb of sadness hung over the home. The loss of a much-loved companion was bad enough, but when that companion was also their gifted and generous top dog it was almost too much to bear. Despite the strong pack leadership of the Alpha-Pair, at grass roots level grief and aimlessness inevitably led to squabbles and this particular morning was no exception. The remaining pack members were huddled around the Aga in the kitchen sharing memories about Joey and his exploits, but they now lapsed into a sad silence.

"I knew Joey when I was just a pup, long before I came here."

Destiny scowled and stared across at Pippa who faced her with an injured air.

"So?"

"You don't seem to think I miss him, yet I've known him longer than you!"

Pippa met Destiny's gaze full-on and refused to drop hers in submission. Since getting her paws under the table Pippa was proving to be a confident and determined little bitch with a big heart and a stubborn streak who coveted Destiny's position of power.

"I've never said anything of the sort," Destiny protested, drawing herself upright in indignation. However, the others did not miss the sudden blink of acknowledgement and the pinkness that was creeping around her muzzle.

"No, you just cut me out – every time! Doesn't she girls?" Pippa appealed to Flossie and Fenella who now accepted their rank beneath her in the pack hierarchy. Flossie and Fenella said nothing, but exchanged looks and sidled closer to Pippa for support.

"She's right, Destiny," Flossie dared suddenly, sticking out a mutinous and stubborn lip. "And it's not fair!" she added with a sudden flare of unusual hostility.

"Are you challenging my authority, Flossie?" Destiny said icily.

The ensuing silence crackled with tension and Flossie and Fenella looked anxiously at one another whilst Clifford blinked, sat up straight and stuck out his left ear as was his way during stressful situations. This usually brought forth some laughter as the others said it was Clifford's way of saying, 'left turn, I'm outa here!' but nobody smiled today.

"I think we all just forgot that Pippa knew Uncle Joey before coming here."

It was Fenella, the little Omega member who had spoken, and mindful of her role as Pack Peacemaker, she met Destiny's gaze without fear. They all held their breath and waited for the storm to break, but it never came.

"Yes, that's it. We just forgot," Destiny conceded curtly, but obviously grateful for Fenella's face-saving intervention. "He had a soft spot for you too, Pippa," she added, with a flash of sudden generosity.

"That's probably because he felt guilty! He hated me hanging off his ears and used to grumble and chase me off!" Pippa said with a sad little smile.

"If only D'Arcy was here," Tickle whispered in the midst of their grief. "He would know what to do."

She paused in the rhythmic and continual licking of one front paw, a distress signal that had begun the day Joey left, then carried on licking. They had been so close; especially during the latter days when she refused to leave Joey's side except to toilet. There was now a cold and empty space on the big bed that had been his, and which she usually left her own bed to share. "All this arguing and falling out, D'Arcy should be here to take over," she whispered, for once looking her age with face drawn and eyes red in the depths of her grief. Her years now sat heavily upon her and heaving a big sigh, she closed her eyes and gave into this new and crushing weariness. The Pack members fell silent and looked shamefacedly at one another.

"What are we thinking of, carrying on like this when Tickle needs us?" Destiny whispered, shaking her head in remorse. Crossing to Tickle's side, she snuffled her ear and murmured words of comfort. Pippa and Clifford watched her with anxiety clouding their faces whilst Flossie and Fenella exchanged worried looks. Despite her great age, Tickle's strength and resilience were legendary and could be relied upon in any crisis. It was a shock to see her in this weakened state, and her helplessness at the loss of Joey made them all feel frightened and vulnerable.

"We're sorry, Ticks, we'll all pull together and look after you," Clifford said with a quiver in his voice, looking round at the others for support.

"Yes, yes of course we will, won't we girls?" Destiny piped up, careful this time to include Pippa as she looked at Flossie and Fenella. The youngsters nodded shyly in agreement and moved closer to Pippa for comfort. Bereavement was new to them and they were unsure of what to say and how to conduct themselves, and felt smothered by the blanket of darkness and sadness that had draped itself over the Pack.

"And I'll look after your girls for you," Pippa said to Destiny with a new respect in her demeanour, "so that you can stay close to Nan Tickle and give her comfort."

Destiny nodded and blinked twice in acknowledgement of this concession.

"You have to keep going for *us*, Tickle," Destiny said shrewdly, sensing a dark angel hovering over their Pack Nanny.

"Yes. Yes, of course." Tickle had opened her eyes to resume the endless licking. Preoccupied with her memories she paid little attention to their talk.

Destiny and Clifford exchanged worried looks: instead of looking half her age as usual, Tickle, drawn and faded as she was by grief, looked every one of her thirteen years.

"Destiny has it right Tickle, we can't move on without you," Clifford said urgently, his huge dark eyes larger than ever and filmed with sadness and something like fear.

Tickle sighed and carried on licking.

Later, as they drank at the trough outside the kitchen door, Flossie whispered to her sister

"I heard Alpha-She say it was a worrying time and that they must keep an eye on Tickle."

"Why, what did she mean?" Fenella asked, eyebrows creased in perplexity and water streaming from her mouth as she raised her head to gaze at Flossie, then shook it hard and sent droplets cascading over her sister, an event that usually raised an indignant protest but which today passed without comment.

"In case she decided to follow Uncle Joey."

"Oh no!" Fenella's mouth drooped in sadness. "She mustn't do it! It's bad enough losing our Top Dog, without losing our Pack Nanny too! She has to stay for our sake. You must tell her Flossie!"

"It won't make any difference, not if she's made up her mind," Flossie said knowledgeably.

"Can you die just like that, because you want to?" Fenella asked, looking sceptical.

"I think it's more about losing the will to live than wanting to die."

"That's very wise, Flossie."

They both started and whirled round to face Destiny who had appeared behind them.

"It happened to Grandsire Ben once didn't it?" Fenella piped up, not wanting to appear naïve. "I remember you telling the story Destiny, about the Spirit of the Water and how you saved him and your brother."

"Only with a lot of help, Fenella, that's why we must rally round Tickle." Destiny's eyes took on the clouded far-off look that every pack member recognised as she acknowledged some secret debt. She frowned and sighed at the same time as though confused and perplexed.

"I wonder what that was about?" Fenella asked as Destiny returned indoors to sit with Tickle.

"I reckon it was something to do with D'Arcy," Flossie whispered. These days she had given up referring to him as 'Uncle' deeming herself too grown up for the practice, and Destiny accepted or challenged this presumption depending on mood and circumstance.

"How?"

"I don't know exactly, but she has always stood against D'Arcy going away."

"We're not supposed to know about that. But I think you're right; the memory of that story made her realise something," Fenella said quietly. "Maybe it reminded her that what we all see as bad is also good," she added.

"What are you banging on about, sis?" Flossie demanded. Ever the practical one, a dismissive air served to cover up ignorance whenever strange notions arose and floated beyond her grasp like dandelion seeds on the wind. Fenella was staring beyond her, out over the garden to the shadows of the wood behind.

"I think it's about Grey Pelt," Fenella whispered, dropping her voice still further as she uttered the name.

"How? What you mean, Fenella? In any case, you shouldn't speak about him, you know it's forbidden!" Flossie floundered on this unfamiliar ground, but Fenella had turned and was trotting back into the house.

Flossie stared after her, with the same uncomfortable feeling that, on certain occasions, her Aunt Destiny aroused.

Rosa Just Joey: for which Joey was named

A strange light appears outside the grotto

11.

Visitations

Meanwhile, in a grotto deep in the forest at the foot of the mountain which he had managed to reach before nightfall, D'Arcy stirred and twitched in uneasy sleep. It seemed he heard his beloved Nan Tickle crying and moaning and felt her near-death weakness. He sensed too the chill of emptiness at her side and whimpered pitifully in his sleep. He awoke before dawn, bone-chilled and with his mind hazed by mist and memory and troubled by a sorrow he could not name. His shoulders shifted beneath the invisible burden he carried. It lay heavier upon them now, as the new weight of leadership descended and finally made itself felt.

Joey! Joey, mate!

A cold hand reached inside D'Arcy's chest and clutched at his heart.

I have to go back!

No sooner had the thought arisen than he was on his feet, despite the pain from his wound which was beginning to fester. Yet he stood for a time unmoving; mesmerized by what he saw. Ice-fangs hung down in a menacing row along the edge of the overhang, but something far stranger caught his attention. Beyond the mouth of the cave snow swirled, shot through with the grey of dawn and a luminescence of silver that shimmered like the watered silk of Alpha-She's best blouse. The beloved image this conjured up brought a rush of nostalgia and longing. *I have to go home*, he thought, suddenly forlorn.

Yet as he watched, still transfixed, it seemed a dark shadow was forming at the centre of the light, framed by a halo of silver. His heart leapt in his chest as first the strong body then noble head began to take shape, and he half expected to see Joey enter the cave at a trot as though doing his winning lap of the show ring (as was his way whenever he moved). But this coat was of pewter rather than gold, he realised squinting into the fug, and the head that appeared in the midst of the halo, despite the hazing of form and light-frazzled line, was unmistakable.

"Ben!" D'Arcy breathed, and he lowered his head and sank down in submission to his timeless leader.

You can do nothing for Joey by going back.

The image wavered to and fro like a candle flame in a passing breath; ethereal and indistinct, it hovered at the entrance, the words not exactly spoken aloud yet D'Arcy nevertheless knew he had heard them. He crouched on the rough ground, terrified yet with a strange sense of comfort too because he was no longer alone with his troubles.

I must go back; Tickle is giving up and Death is moving closer.

The words were thought rather than spoken yet it seemed the apparition at the mouth of the cave instantly read his mind.

Joey will help Tickle. You must stay with the Quest – that is your burden and you must carry it bravely, no matter what.

The note of authority was also unmistakable and D'Arcy, relieved of his dilemma and the need to make a decision, bowed his head in acquiescence.

"But I've let everyone down by not being there, especially Joey."

D'Arcy's misery and sense of failure washed over him in a bitter tide. The image at the centre of the vortex throbbed with light and energy.

You will let more than the Pack down if you desert your mission; it reaches beyond us to affect the lives of all our kind – and others too. The timing is as it should be. Had I been sent for Joey whilst you were there, as new Top Dog you would not have felt able to leave. Do you doubt my judgement D'Arcy?

"Never." D'Arcy shook his head with vehemence. If there had been any doubts at all in his mind that this really was his Grandsire Ben, they now disappeared like smoke from a guttered candle. "But I am not you, Ben. I have failed not only my Pack but Grey Pelt too because I lack your strength and power."

I know you carry him within you D'Arcy, but I am there too – twice-fold.

D'Arcy raised his head a fraction, eyes sad and lack-lustre. "How is that?"

Because I am not only in your genes, but in your soul.

D'Arcy fell silent for several minutes and his forehead crinkled with the effort of thinking. "But your soul and mine are separate surely."

Only partly. One evening a month or so after I passed over Rainbow Bridge and you were little more than a yearling, you took ill and collapsed without warning. You were standing next to Alpha-She and slid to the floor unconscious. Alpha-She was demented, thinking she was about to lose you too. I picked up on her distress and your out-of-body condition, and gave you some of my new Life-force to keep you alive. By the time the emergency vet-man arrived you had struggled to your feet. You still have that soul-force within you and always will have.

"You saved my life," D'Arcy breathed, awestruck. "But I don't remember anything of what happened that night."

It had to happen that way in order for me to enter.

"But why me?" D'Arcy leaned closer as the image began to fade and the light grow almost imperceptibly fainter. "Is it connected with Grey Pelt and the Quest?" he asked urgently. "Where am I going, and what have I to do?"

He had to strain to hear the next words as they were garbled and indistinct as though coming through the ether from far away.

I have to go now D'Arcy. Keep faith and you will succeed.

The image began to blur and fragment like trees and rocks when viewed through a rain-splattered window, and finally disappeared leaving D'Arcy alone once more.

As dawn tinged the night sky with grey, Tickle lay on her bed fitfully sleeping. Destiny, who was also wakeful having sensed something strange happening to her brother, noticed how Tickle's paws and whiskers were twitching and, as though party to a forbidden secret, something suspiciously like a smile came to her lips.

Tickle blinked twice and asked herself if she was dreaming. The golden aura that had appeared by the kitchen door grew stronger. A familiar, much-loved and scarce-believed shape was forming at its centre.

"Joey?" she whispered, her heart beginning to thump inside her plump white breast.

"Yes, Tickle, it's me."

"But how, why . . .?" Tickle began to tremble so much she could not finish the sentence. Joey's image fragmented and receded, then congealed and advanced again but it was undeniably him.

"It's okay Ticks. No need to worry. I came to tell you to stop fretting!"

"But how is it possible?" Tickle didn't know whether she was vaguely disappointed that this Joey didn't act remotely angelic and speak words of great wisdom, or be delighted that he was just the same old down-to-earth boy.

"Well I'm pretty new to all this," he confessed, "which is why I keep jiggling about and fading, but your distress summoned me here. I was allowed to come because you are such a fine Pack Nanny and had a deep need. I don't think I'm doing too bad actually." Joey sat upright and puffed out his chest in the way that Tickle remembered so well.

"You're doing fine Joey," she said, smiling and wiping away a tear at the same time. "It's so wonderful to see you and know you are all right. Am I allowed to tell the others?"

"You can, but they won't believe you Ticks, they'll nod their heads and exclaim 'how wonderful!' then behind your back whisper 'she was just dreaming, you know.' But *you'll* know it was real."

"How will I know that? This might just be a lovely dream," Tickle whispered, doubt and sadness clouding her eyes.

"Keep your eyes and mind open Tickle, and listen to Alpha-She. In return you must be strong again – for me! As Elder and Guardian you must take over until D'Arcy returns."

"But what about Clifford!"

"Clifford is a great lad, and one day the pack will have his son to carry on Ben's name and looks. But he is not a top dog, nor does he want to be one. Destiny will lead the girls and be your acting top bitch, but she can be a tad abrasive and during this awful time could trigger a rebellion. So you must take the lead Nan Tickle and save my pack for me!"

"I'll try, Joey, I'll try."

"Do it, and I promise you will know this is real. Listen to Alpha-*She, She, She, Sh* . . ." As he spoke, Joey's voice grew fainter, and the light that surrounded his image dimmed, until finally there was nothing but silence and darkness. But feelings of warmth and love remained.

Tickle rested her head on her paws and drifted into a deep and healing sleep.

Meanwhile, D'Arcy left his scrape of a bed, awakened by pain and hunger. He had crawled back there to think about what had just taken place, and had eventually drifted into a half-sleep. Weakened also by the severe cold he crept outside into a white world of emptiness. Hunger pangs gnawed at his stomach and his head buzzed with weakness so that it was hard to focus, but the smell of warm flesh and blood drove him forward and filled his mouth with juices. He followed his nose and also his eyes as tendrils of steam rose and hung on the air, betraying the place. A snow-dusted rabbit this time, and pair of plump pigeons, lay on snow that was spotted with fresh bloodstains. If there had been any paw prints they were now covered. D'Arcy knew he should look about him, be cautious of this fresh offering and a prey that was abnormally large and unusual for Hushwing, but was past caring. So who could have left it? The question did briefly cross his mind before he fell upon the food and began ravenously to devour it.

Restored by his meal and his thirst slaked by crashing his paw through the skin of ice that covered the beck, he began to cleanse his wounds, licking each puncture and spitting out the foul-tasting pus. He knew the infection was deepening and spreading down his leg, but also that he had to move on. He set off at a slow pace, but making some progress by keeping to the exposed parts where the snow had partially frozen and was hard and crunchy. At times he staggered up to his shoulders in soft drifts, and at such times was tempted to lie down, fall asleep – and die. Yet he was driven on by an unknown force to an indefinite destination. He knew only that he had to cross the mountain that loomed before him, barring his way.

As he limped on the sun nudged its way over the horizon and rose in the clear blue sky. The land was transformed into a winking, blinking blaze of colour as ice-crystals caught and refracted pinpoints of light. Dazzled he dipped his head and with eyes screwed up against the glare plodded on. His eyes flew wide and hackles rose at a sudden movement in one of the stunted trees that were becoming sparser with every foot he climbed. He relaxed again as a bird alighted on another branch and sent a shower of snow cascading down. He stood and watched the sparkling cloud as it drifted slowly through sunlight to earth. The tiny prisms within flashed and twinkled with ice-fire, alight with red, blue, green and all the colours of the rainbow. *Like the two stones in the ring that Alpha-She always wore on her finger.* Thoughts of her constricted his chest and made it difficult to breathe. He thought then too of Ben and all he had imparted: he had to carry on and overcome if he was to see his beloved Alpha again. This would be the spur to keep him going – and alive. With this in mind he set off again, bunching his chest and foreleg muscles to pull himself upward and ease the strain on his wounded haunch. Judgement was all now: either he must find shelter on this flank of the mountain, or the summit would have to be reached before nightfall and a safe place sought on descent of the other side. If night fell as he neared the summit, there would be no turning back in time and on that bare and exposed space he would surely perish.

The sun continued to shine throughout the day and despite exhaustion and the pain of his hindquarters, D'Arcy made good progress. He was fast approaching the Rubicon and would soon have to make that life or death decision of whether to hole up for the night or continue. He looked anxiously up at the sky, judging how long he had left by the position of the sun as it reddened and sank towards the western horizon. Long enough, he decided. The sheep track he was following made progress easier and quicker and he had a good chance of reaching the summit before night fall. Even so the way was hard, and as time passed what little heat the sun had given became hazed by mist and distance. As the temperature fell the snow began to freeze and paws and claws struggled to get a grip, impeding his progress. He was tiring. The red ball of the sun was sinking now and the sky was streaked with blood. The summit loomed before him. It was too late to turn back.

Tickle awoke with a little cry as she left a disturbing dream in which D'Arcy was a pup again and crying out to her because he was hurt, then relaxed again as she breathed in the calming oils of lavender and chamomile left by Alpha-She in the little dish on the Aga. She did this each night during these troubled times, to soothe their worries and induce a healing sleep. She lay half asleep, thinking of Joey's visit and wondering if she would still believe it the following morning or recognise it as just a comforting dream. Whatever it was, the night now seemed less dark, the future less bleak, and she was grateful enough for that. Then her sleepy thoughts turned again to D'Arcy, and love poured out for her lost boy. Wherever he was, she prayed that the Great Mother would keep him safe and warm and send him safely back to them when his Quest was done. The love and hope that now warmed Tickle's being seeped out beyond her and flowed forth.

He stood alone on the summit, chilled and exhausted but filled with a sense of achievement. As he gazed out over the snowy fells and bloodstained sky he thought of Ben's promise that he would send Joey to comfort Tickle. Thoughts of Tickle brought a flush of warmth and surge of new strength to his body and limbs, and he knew he could make the descent into the dire place they called Weirdale before night closed in.

On the edge of Weirdale Forest

12.

D'Arcy enters the forest and Tickle finds the truth

He did indeed make the dangerous descent before nightfall, albeit slipping and sliding most of the way and with little to spare in the way of twilight. He paused several times on the way down to raise his head and sniff the frost-bound air. His nostrils twitched and hackles rose as he tasted a faint but disturbing odour. Exhausted and with bleeding pads but aware of the need to find shelter for the night, he searched beneath a sky of glittering stars that promised another severe frost. He came upon a hollow beneath the trunk of a tree that had fallen to the gales of the previous month, its branches resting on a boulder to create a shelter below. He crept beneath and slept at first from exhaustion, then fitfully due to cold and apprehension. That unidentified odour had twitched at more than his nostrils, it had resurrected a long-lost memory that clung to his mind like a cobweb in broken and incomplete strands. Once he awoke and fancied he heard a faint keening and howling that chilled his blood then, as the sound faded, decided it must have been the shrieking of Hushwing on the hunt. The silence that fell was profound and he began to think he had imagined it. He hunched up against the freezing cold, tucked his nose beneath his tail to warm and circulate the air he breathed and drifted into uneasy sleep.

It was a grim and inhospitable valley in which D'Arcy found himself at daybreak. Emerging from his temporary shelter he shivered, surveyed the white wilderness that stretched before him and his head drooped in dejection. He quailed before this land of rocky terrain and snow-filled gullies towered over by a range of bare and austere mountains. A bitter north wind had arisen; it moaned through the valley, the sound amplified and distorted by the walls of rock that hemmed in the dalehead, to be thrown back again as disquieting echoes. It was a bleak, lonesome sound that filled D'Arcy with a deep ache and longing for home. The icy blast rattled the bare branches of oak and rowan and soughed through tall conifers with a swishing sound like that of waves on the shore. Riding on its back were flurries of snow and he shivered afresh and wondered what on earth had driven him to this desolate place. Hunger gnawed at his belly and he was overcome by a wave of faintness and weakness. Whatever he had heard last night it was not likely to be Hushwing – unless she had forsaken him, for there was no fresh kill left for him this morning. Regardless, he would have to move on and find a better place to hide out.

At the time that D'Arcy was thinking of finding a more permanent hide, Tickle sought a moment or two of solitude in which to try and make sense of events. Was D'Arcy safe? Had he found shelter from the bitter cold, or had he already perished? She was sitting alone outside their home on a patch of grass from which the morning sunlight had melted the frost. She was gazing up at the snow-covered Misty Mountain and trying to imagine where D'Arcy might be and whether he was surviving. A worried frown furrowed her forehead and her eyes filled with sadness at the loss of her boy. This in turn brought her to that other loss and thoughts of Joey, and the mysterious events of the night before. Had it really happened? she questioned herself, did Joey really visit her or had it merely been a dream?

So engrossed was she with these questions that she didn't notice the robin hopping across the grass towards her until it halted a mere leash-length away and cocked its head to one side. Her attention caught by the movement, she stared at the tiny bird thinking it was either stupid or had a death wish. Suddenly, it hopped forward a couple of paces and, unbelievably, landed on her left paw. She stared at it, too incredulous to make a snap. It stared back at her its black shiny eyes holding her mesmerised. That this should happen to her, Tickle of the keenest game sense and scourge of the garden birds! Before she could decide what move to make, the back door opened and Alpha-She leaned out. "Time for breakfast, Tickle," she called. Immediately the robin flew up in the air and disappeared over the shrubbery. Still puzzling over this unlikely occurrence, Tickle rose and trotted indoors.

"You know what they say, don't you, Tickle," Alpha-She said as she passed, and Tickle looked up inquiringly at her. "That birds are the messengers of the soul. Either that robin is kamikaze or Joey was telling you something," she said with a sad little smile as she closed the door.

But Tickle was jubilant. He had let her know! Joey had given her an unmistakable sign just as he promised, and not only that, he had confirmed it through Alpha-She! *Listen to Alpha-She,* Joey had said. And after that pesky robin had spooked her out, what did Alpha-She come out with but 'birds are messengers of the soul' and she had even mentioned Joey! That morning Tickle not only ate her breakfast but, ravenous from not eating for several days, pumped her forepaw up and down to ask for more. The pack whispered in corners, noting her upbeat mood and sudden return of vitality. When pressed, she told them about Joey coming to her in the night, and just as he had predicted, they nodded and touched her paw and said kindly, 'how lovely Ticks', but she knew by the way they stopped talking or changed the subject whenever she appeared, and by the overheard whispers *'whatever, it has done the trick; kinder to let her believe it'* that they assumed it had just been a dream.

Tickle simply smiled serenely to herself and whispered 'Thank you, Joey' and went on her untroubled way. From that day she ate well, gained strength and her spirits rose. The others, if not exactly happy and care-free, began to settle and function as a pack once more and help each other move on. Joey had passed over Rainbow Bridge and nothing could change that fact. D'Arcy too was still missing, but the Nanny Tickle they knew and loved had returned to guide the Pack. Her strength, kindness and wisdom inspired new hope and the belief that all was not lost.

The day wore on and despite foraging until weary D'Arcy found nothing edible nor a suitable place to hole up that night. His wounds were throbbing and every step forward cost him a shaft of red hot pain that blurred his vision and filled him with nausea, so that even had he been inclined to shed blood, which – being a sensitive gentle soul – he was not, there was little hope of catching a bird or rodent. To eat the result of somebody else's kill was hard enough, and only extreme hunger had made the fresh blood and still warm flesh palatable. Given this situation the

Pack's Bitches would have no such qualms, he reflected, a trifle shamefaced. Destiny in particular would soon hunt, kill and provide her pack with sustenance. Eventually, driven by the age-old and strong survival instinct, he made a couple of stumbling attempts at catching a bird but failed miserably. His intended prey flew off discharging a volley of indignant cries whilst a couple of rooks cawed their derision at his incompetence. D'Arcy crumpled; without food to fuel body-heat the intense cold would claim him and he would lose all sense of direction and reality.

He dragged on, sick with pain, aching with cold and griped by hunger pains until he could go no further. Both will and physical energy were depleted beyond recall. There were no more thoughts of failure, or even of returning to the Pack, only the desire to succumb to this will-sapping weariness and craving for sleep. The snow felt soft and warm now that he had given up the fight. At length he crept into a snow-filled depression, lay down and closed his eyes. He was vaguely aware that he may not wake up again, but no longer cared.

He was sinking fast into a warm, dark place from which there could be no return, but something was pulling him back. A strange yet also familiar scent was twitching at his nostrils but his eyelids were too heavy to prise open. The crunch of paws on crisp snow moving in his direction vaguely registered. Then the sound ceased and he was aware of a presence close-by. Something of the survival instinct still smouldered within and a small flame of self-preservation flared. With difficulty he prised open his lids and the sight that met his eyes made it impossible for him to close them again. He must either have already perished, or be dreaming the dream of the near-dead. A splendid creature stood motionless before him, hazed by the dying light of day. The pelt of bronze and gold was tinged with a rosy hue cast by the setting sun, and dusted with snow from the branches disturbed by the noble head. A pair of slanted and startling blue eyes watched him without blinking.

D'Arcy watched transfixed as the vision shifted, advanced and receded from his failing sight. An ancestral spirit had come for him, to escort him over the Rainbow Bridge, was his immediate thought. There were no wolves here and had not been for a long time now; Alpha-She had told them. He sniffed the air and recognised her scent as that of a female. The odour was warm and sensual, too real to be that of a phantom. This she-wolf was also young and therefore probably of low rank and hopefully not about to attack. He blinked twice and lowered his head again to show respect for being on her territory and a lack of hostile intent. Ears laid back in suspicion, she continued to stare that unnerving stare and he dropped his gaze so as not to antagonise. He tried to lift a paw but was too weak. Seeing this, she advanced slowly, one foot raised and poised before placing the other, much as she might stalk her prey. His heart thumped in his chest; cold, hunger and fever took their toll and the world went black.

He awoke to unaccustomed warmth and a weight along his flank. It was several minutes before he could make sense of this, but when he turned his head, he realised with a tremor of shock that the she-wolf was warming him with her own body. Not daring further movement, he gazed into those luminous blue eyes so perfectly outlined with black. She rose immediately and stood a few paces away watching him, ears thrust back and tail pointing straight out and ready for any show of hostility. D'Arcy looked away and lowered his head again in submission. Should she choose to attack, even without his wounds, he would have no chance against this fanged and sturdily built stranger.

"Why should I warm you and then attack?" she said with a scornful expression and a strong dialect that he struggled to understand.

"I didn't, I mean—" he stuttered weakly and lapsed into silence from the effort of speaking. It seemed what they said about wolves being mystical creatures was at least partly true; she appeared to have read his thoughts. In this she reminded him of his sister and he was gripped by pangs of longing.

"I read your body language," she added, a gleam of something like amusement in her eyes.

"Thank you for saving my life. But why should you do that when we are natural enemies?" he gasped, his breath shallow and painful in his chest.

"We are not. It is Man that has made us enemies not Nature."

"But why stay with me now?"

She remained still and watchful, head to one side as though considering whether to answer. "I recognised your mark," she said at last, in a voice so low it was almost a whisper. She cast a quick glance over her shoulder as though afraid of being overheard. She lifted her head and sniffed the air several times and as though satisfied, turned to look at him again.

"Then you must have been chosen too. Blue eyes – is that your mark?" D'Arcy dared.

Her nose wrinkled again. "You stink," she said bluntly before he could finish. Then aware he was about to insist on an answer she added, "you have a wound that has gone bad." She moved swiftly to his side and he winced as she found and nosed the injured flank. "We have to get you to shelter, then we can clean you up and you can explain what you are doing in our territory," she said brusquely, and with that strange intonation that he was beginning to follow. "Can you walk?" she added, nudging his rear with her nose so that the pain made him shift and struggle to his feet.

"I can try."

"It is not far. Follow me."

D'Arcy did so, and however strange his guide, he also derived comfort from watching her lope ahead, pausing now and then to look over her shoulder and check that he was still following, and slackening her pace as necessary. Stumbling in a dream-like state at her rear, he noted the proud stature, the confidence of the paced stride, and above all the strong dark pattern marking neck and spine and knew that his immediate impression of a low-ranking female had been entirely mistaken. In following her it seemed, fanciful though it may be, that he was also following his destiny. *Is this the reason I have been brought here to this desolate place?* he wondered. Any thoughts of how a creature driven by Man from every corner of this Land came to be there were overlaid by the need to stay on his feet and survive.

She led him to a hidden dell deep in the forest that covered an area of the dalehead. Huge boulders piled against the foothills at their back. These led to the sheer flank of the mountain ridge that formed one side of this steep-sided valley gouged and scoured by Nature during the last ice-age. She pushed aside an overhang of conifer branches and ivy to reveal the entrance to a shallow cave. Even in his weakened and fevered state, D'Arcy saw that not only would this provide a safe place for the night, but also serve as a more permanent base. Following her lead he crawled thankfully inside.

Moon-song

13.

Wolf-wisdom

The hour or so that followed would be remembered by D'Arcy as some magical and impossible dream. Using her teeth the she-wolf tugged aside strands of ivy to allow the last light of day to spill into the darkness of the cave. Obeying her instruction to stretch out on his good side on the soft earth, he watched and flinched as she punctured the festering flesh of his wounds and nibbled at putrid tissue to release the evil-smelling pus.

"Who shot you? There are three or four pellets in here," she said matter-of-factly.

"A farmer thought I was worrying his sheep, but I was just passing through," he gasped through his agony. "His dogs caught my scent and set after me."

"You were lucky. That chase took you almost out of range! But these pellets have to come out."

She probed and licked until he almost fainted, then spat out each pellet in turn onto to the dirt floor. Her tongue then worked rhythmically to cleanse the open wounds and she periodically coughed and spat out the poison. The fiery pain was almost more than he could bear and a groan or two escaped but careful of his pride and manhood, he refrained from calling out.

"Where did you learn this?" he asked, curious despite his pain.

"I am the Pack Healer," she answered shortly, and carried on working in silence.

"Does that make you special?"

"You have courage," she said ignoring the question, and paused in licking the wounds to give him respite and to ask in her strange tongue "Your collar and well-fed look tell me you live with humans. What do they call you?"

"D'Arcy."

"H'mmmm." She sat back on her haunches watching him. "I like that."

"What do they call you?"

"I am Moon-song."

"That is beautiful," D'Arcy mumbled, suddenly embarrassed, perhaps because he wanted to add 'like you' but added instead "But I smell human on you too!"

"Man brought us here. The Alpha-Pair and their son and daughter and an unrelated pair were born in captivity. They were released into this valley and Man provided food and protection until they were able to hunt and fend for themselves. They made wolf sounds to teach the Alpha-Pair about the different kinds of howling and what they mean, and how to survive in the wild. When the Alpha-Pair settled, they began to breed and I was born. But several times a year the humans come to check on us, and leave us an extra kill in the harsh weather, like now, which is why I carry their scent from the carcase."

"Why the two unrelated wolves?"

"It was hoped they would spilt off eventually and form a pack of their own."

"And did they?"

111

"Yes, this Autumn gone." The answer was curt and the tone discouraged further probing of the subject.

"Is this your den?" he asked instead.

"I only come here when I need to think. I live with the Pack on the other side of the valley. Normally we sleep in the open. My winter coat is much thicker than yours and is defence enough against the cold," she added as D'Arcy grimaced. "It seals in our body heat; snow will not melt on a wolf coat! Yours is very fine – but bred for vanity not protection!" Then seeing his affronted expression she smiled and added, "It is beautiful, but not suited to life in the wild."

"But I thought wolves lived in dens."

"The underground den is only in use during birthing and rearing the cubs. You must not go anywhere near though."

"They would set on me." It was a statement not a question.

"Our Alpha-male has to protect the pack territory and den. He may attack, especially if he found you with me."

"Are you his mate?" D'Arcy asked, suddenly afraid.

"No, a daughter. Only the Alpha-pair are allowed to mate, and then they only produce what the pack and its territory can support. But mating time is drawing near and Granite, our Alpha-male, is even more possessive than usual on account of Blackthorn the new Alpha-male. But that's enough for now – D'Arcy," her tongue stumbled over the unaccustomed name but he thrilled to hear it spoken by this mysterious stranger. "I must go."

"No! Please, don't leave me here alone!" He cringed, aware of the pleading note in his voice, but the thought of being left here alone was too much to bear.

"I shall return."

With that she left abruptly.

As she disappeared he crawled to the entrance and looked out into the gathering twilight. He watched, frowning and perplexed, as she rolled from side to side in the snow before rising to her feet and loping off into the distance, then realised she was ridding herself of his scent before returning to the pack. Desolate, he returned to his bed on the soft earth and also realised why she had left so suddenly. As the first moonbeams filtered in through the gap in the overhang, a thin, high wail reached his ears, followed by a different voice and tone, and yet another overlapping the first then the whole rising and falling plaintively on the twilight. It was, he marvelled, more like human singing than dog-sound. Her ultra sensitive hearing had picked up the rising notes before him, for his senses had been blunted by easy living. The howling haunted his soul and brought an ache of recognition to his heart. And it was calling her home too. Perhaps at the core they were not so different after all.

The keening stopped and silence descended, broken only by the twit-twit-te-e-w-o-o of a tawny owl on the hunt. It brought to mind Hushwing and the realisation that her unearthly shrieks had been absent for some time now. Then he stiffened as a second howling was set up, but the voices had changed, were issued from different throats. This, he realised, must be the howling of the secondary pack. Was it the reason for her abruptness and change of subject when asked about it? Had the new offshoot pack proved a challenge to the original one? He would see what he could prise from her when – *if* – she returned. But he dare not consider the possibility of her not returning, and what would happen to him in that eventuality

During this eventful time the Pack members back home were rallying to Tickle's new strength and vitality. However, it was during the evening lull that distress at D'Arcy's continued absence was most keenly felt. The Alpha-Pair had done everything they could to bring about his return but to no avail.

"I heard them talking yesterday," Fenella whispered as a drawn and sad-eyed Alpha-She picked up their dinner dishes and bore them away to be washed.

"Alpha-He said he had talked to the police again and given them D'Arcy's chip details and description. Alpha-She said she had put a notice in the paper promising a reward to anyone helping to find him."

"Does that include me? I'm off then up that mountain!" Flossie quipped, then shrank from embarrassment at the glares of disapproval.

"She was only trying to make us smile and feel better," Destiny said in resigned tones. The others looked at one another with raised eyebrows: Destiny had mellowed much over the past few weeks.

Clifford sighed and sat up straight, stretched his spine, then slumped in misery. "I can't understand why he would go – and stay away like this. Especially, well you know, with Joey . . ." He left the sentence unfinished and his eyes filled with sadness; Joey had been Clifford's best friend and protector for many a year and his passing had hit him hard. For the first time he had to think and act for himself and this filled him with worry and insecurity.

"He doesn't know about Joey going," Flossie said, always the practical sensible one and quick to recover from any set-down.

"But he's still staying away from us," Pippa said sadly. She had nursed a fondness for the big handsome boy since the day of her arrival.

"He must have his reasons," Tickle said firmly, "and we must trust him."

"Well yes, but he has left us to cope at the worst possible time, while he goes off on some wild adventure," Clifford grumbled, looking up at the ceiling and sticking out his left ear.

"And you would think he would at least find a way to get word to us that he is okay, and intends to return," Pippa added, nodding agreement.

"It is out of his hands; he has to follow the call and obey the rules of the Quest."

It was Fenella who had spoken out, and she exchanged a knowing look with Destiny before sinking down and turning away her head to hide her sudden embarrassment at being the focus of the Pack's attention.

Destiny looked from one to another as the bickering continued. A worried frown creased her forehead as though she was deliberating over a weighty decision. She appeared to make up her mind and stretched and sat upright again.

"I feel a song coming on!" she declared.

"No Destiny!" Clifford began to protest looking scared, but his voice was drowned by the enthusiastic chorus that greeted Destiny's announcement.

Destiny sat very still, waiting for the words to come from out there into her head. The rest of the Pack waited in silence. This home was full of them: the voices of those who had been called away but could not bear to wholly leave it. It was there in the background, an incessant stream of words mumbling over the stones of the Pack's existence. And Destiny could hear it. Her reputation as Pack Poet and Bard was well earned. She began to sing in a high voice beyond the pitch of human ears.

> In the corner of your eye
> On the cobweb of a dream,
> These things are often sensed
> But only rarely seen.
> The creature round the corner,
> The breath that stains the night
> On a frost-bitten evening
> With nobody in sight.
>
> It's a shadow on the sunlight
> A wisp across the moon,
> Blink or try to focus and
> It disappears too soon.
> It shudders in the lightning
> And in the thunder booms,
> It crackles in the firelight
> And in the darkness looms.

In the bat-squeaks of twilight
Or when the Dawn Chorus sings,
You can catch it in the rainbow
Of a dragon-fly's wings.
It is the meaning in the spaces
Of a language without words
That is heard in falling raindrops
And the whirring wings of birds.

Grasp the blinking of an eye
Or the weaving of a dream,
Clutch the spinning of a cobweb
To capture what I mean.
Those whose inner eye is open
Will learn and understand,
But there's folly in this wisdom
For he is His now to command!

As she sang that last line, Destiny sat up very straight and looked hard at each one of them in turn, as if willing them to understand.

"You mean D'Arcy, don't you?" Clifford asked, his voice and demeanour subdued.

"Is that what Tickle meant about trusting him? That there are things you and D'Arcy understand that we don't?" Flossie contributed.

"Destiny is telling us to stop sitting in judgement of D'Arcy because he is undergoing an ordeal," Fenella intervened.

Destiny refused to be drawn, but gave her young niece a nod of approval. "I bring the songs to you; it is for you to give them meaning," she said, turning and walking away. She stood at the French windows, gazing out into the dark, and they sensed the depth of her distress.

Back at the grotto in the glade, the fire in D'Arcy's wounds had cooled since Moon-song's ministrations and removal of the pellets, but he was weakened by fear and hunger. Since being born he had never been left alone; Destiny had always been there at his side, also Alpha-She and the members of the Pack and he had thrived on their love and companionship. Now he lay in the dark completely alone, wishing with all his being that he had never strayed further than the end of the garden. His flanks heaved with distress and his limbs trembled. In fact he had just about given up when the curtain of ivy and branches was pushed aside and Moon-song slipped into the grotto. She was carrying a rabbit in her mouth and dropped it at D'Arcy's feet. Her fangs ripped it open with expertise, and her strong jaws crunched bones with ease to expose the soft flesh and innards. "Eat," she commanded, taking in his near-death exhaustion.

Filled with new hope and revived by sight of his odd but most welcome companion, D'Arcy raised his head and shoulders and crouched, sphinx-like, before the offering. "But I am taking your food," he protested. "It is winter and you need it for yourself."

"No. I have eaten my share of the kill with the pack. I brought this for you."

He bowed his head in thanks and ate slowly at first, nauseated by the smell of fresh meat and warm blood after fasting for so long, then greedily as strength and appetite began to return. Sated, and slightly sickened as she cleared up the remains of his meal, he turned aside and cleaned the blood from his mouth with a forepaw. Feeling a natural urge to go outside after having eaten, he crept out of the cave and relieved himself on the snow. Moon-song followed, and seeing that he was too weak to break the thickening ice on the beck, smashed it for him with a couple of blows. He drank gratefully then raised his head as she loped off into the moon-dappled forest without another word. His heart sank, thinking she was about to leave again so soon and he stood for a time, watching and listening, praying for her return. Weakness and the intense cold drove him back to the entrance of the grotto, but to his intense relief she reappeared, with various stems and leaves grasped in her mouth, and followed him inside.

He sank down exhausted, tiredness tugging at his eyelids now that pain had lessened and the hunger-cramps were relieved, but too joyful at her return to allow himself sleep. "Where did you go?" he asked, watching as she pulled aside the ivy and moonlight cascaded through the gaps to stripe the walls and floor with silver. Instead of answering she began to chew some of the items she had collected. He watched in fascination as she masticated slowly and deliberately, and every now and then made a little cough.

"Lie still." Leaning over him she cleared her throat and spat the pulp of chewed up leaves mixed with mucus and saliva onto his wounds, and spread it gently with her tongue to cover the area. Next she picked up a broad leaf and bruised it by trampling and softening it with her forepaws before placing it over the macerated herb and pressing it down with her tongue. "Move as little as you can," she advised.

"What is it?" he asked, curious.

"Knit-bone. Keep it in place and your wounds will quickly heal and be free of infection."

"Who taught you this?" he asked, amazed by her knowledge.

"I just seem to know."

"You are like my sister, Destiny."

"I like that name too. Is she fey?"

"Very. But feisty and down to earth too, most of the time."

"You are close." It was not a question.

"Yes. I miss her very much. Do you have someone special?" he ventured, and immediately sensed her guard coming up.

"Chew on this, and the pain and heat will go," and she dropped a strip of bark by his head. "It will also give you healing sleep," she added brusquely.

"What is it?"

"You ask a lot of questions, D'Arcy! It is willow bark."

118

She backed away towards the entrance and he sensed her intention to leave.

"You have done so much for me tonight, and without doubt saved my life," he said humbly, then added, "may I beg one more favour?"

"What is it?" she asked, pausing by the curtain of ivy.

"Stay with me until I fall asleep. *Please*," he pleaded un-ashamedly.

She looked taken aback by his request and hesitated before answering, but he noted her ears were forward, her tail hanging down, friendly and relaxed, and he took heart.

"*Only* till you fall asleep," she conceded at last. "But first I must inform the pack that I am hunting this area tonight and will return late."

She slipped past the screen of ivy and through the gap he could see her silhouetted against the waxing moon in a clear frost-brittle sky. The hair along his neck and back quivered and began to rise in anticipation as he watched her throw back her head and open her mouth. The sound that issued forth was one of the most beautiful he had ever heard and he thought how justified was her name. The first note rose on the frost-spangled air, swelling into full-blooded song; more notes followed, rising and falling, billowing and fading, a keening for the souls of slaughtered wolves and a hymn to Lady Moon.

He remained silent when she returned; there was nothing left to say. Her pack had briefly answered her call and all was well. He could have sworn she was smiling as she lay down beside him. Reassured and feeling safer than he had done since leaving the safety of home, D'Arcy fell into a deep and untroubled sleep. But not before the fleeting thought crossed his mind that he was being gently groomed, by one wiser than he in the ways of the Quest.

The Wolves of Weirdale

14.

Avatars and Ancestors

When the snow-reflected light of dawn crept into the grotto where D'Arcy had passed the night in undisturbed sleep, he awoke to a new sensation. In fact the difference was remarkable. His haunch and leg felt sore and a little stiff for sure, but the pain and heat that had raged there for days had now gone. So had the general aching of his body and feeling of illness and melancholy brought on by infection and fever. He marvelled again at Moonsong's knowledge and skill and wondered if he would ever see her again, or whether her work on him now done, she would go her separate way. He found himself fervently hoping it would not be the latter. His body was now healing and he was ravaged by hunger. He rose and tested his leg before moving to the entrance. Somehow he had to find food, or perish. He stepped outside to a silent world blanketed by snow – and the odour of fresh meat. His heart filled with gratitude as he picked up the remains of the pheasant and took it inside. It was so thoughtful of her, he reflected, as he chewed on the meat, to have left this for him knowing he would be hungry on waking. She had done so much for him, and he wondered how he was ever going to repay the debt.

Ben: Delightful naïve boy! He still does not realise why he was brought to this place or the significance of the part he is to play. Moon-song will guide him, and then he will repay the debt – not just to her but all her kind – a hundred times over. But first there are challenges to be faced and overcome . . .

D'Arcy spent the morning exploring and, feeling stronger and fitter, followed Moon-song's tracks through gradually thinning trees to the edge of the forest. Partly concealed behind the massive trunk of an ancient oak he gazed out over the dazzling snow-covered plain and beyond to where the sheer walls of the valley met, apart from a thin winding pass that split the crest, to form the enclosed dalehead. A short distance from the edge of the forest the snow was patterned with paw prints and churned up in places making it impossible to judge the numbers. If he read the signs right, Moon-song's pack had come looking for her and a skirmish of sorts had taken place. He fervently hoped the disturbed snow was evidence rather of a joyful reunion, and that his concern for her safety was misplaced. Nostrils wide, he sniffed and tested the air and recognised the odour that had puzzled and vaguely excited him on first arriving in this valley. It was the powerful musky smell of male wolf mixed with the heady scent of females approaching their oestrus. Instinctively his loins stirred but at the same time a shock of warning ran through him; this was a dangerous time for a mature male dog to be found on wolf territory.

Was that, he thought, turning to leave as he was tired by the morning's exertion, the reason behind the possible skirmish?

Had the males been challenging each other for the right to court Moon-song? He shied away from the strong feeling of aversion to this possibility. He was simply concerned about her safety because she had been so kind, he told himself. The musky scent of a male borne on a northerly wind reached his nostrils and he turned back to investigate. The sight of four adult wolves in the near distance made him move slowly – sudden movements attract attention – behind the trunk of the oak tree again for cover. He crouched there rigid with fear before realising he was upwind of them, and therefore had their scent before they were aware of his presence. They advanced and paused at the centre of the clearing, raising their heads to sniff for prey or intruder. D'Arcy shrank further back into the shadows and prayed they would not see or scent him. If the wind changed direction, he would be in real trouble.

He started as a fifth wolf appeared and slunk towards the group, his almost entirely black pelt stark against the snow. Instantly, their ears were pulled back and tails were held straight out, showing their suspicion of the newcomer's intent. Of the group of wolves the biggest one stood apart in dominant pose, stiff-legged and tall, with ears erect and hackles bristling. That, D'Arcy thought catching his breath, must be Granite, the original pack's Alpha-Male. And I wouldn't like to cross him, he thought, and a shudder rippled his back at the thought. The lone male stalked up to Granite and briefly dipped his head in greeting. D'Arcy wondered at the ranking of this newcomer, as he should have lowered himself completely before the Alpha, then when accepted gently nuzzled him, yet had acted as though of almost equal status. Then a likely explanation dawned: this must be Blackthorn, the new Alpha of the splinter group formed when the pair left the main pack. Judging by the scent and the behaviour of these rival wolves, the new Alpha-Pair would soon mate; but this new and immature Alpha-Male would now be looking for an additional female to produce a second litter, and so quickly increase the size of his pack. It was obvious that his Alpha status at present was token and that he and his mate were subordinate to the main Alpha-Pair. D'Arcy drew in a deep breath and shuddered. He had come upon an explosive situation set to go off at any minute, like the fireworks that fizzed, blazed and pounded the walls of his own valley to celebrate the New Year. Only this situation was far from joyful.

A second male stepped forward and given his position immediately behind the Alpha-Male, was probably the Beta member, trouble-shooter and next in rank. Before D'Arcy could fully realise what was happening, the two younger males were staring hard at one another, tails raised and hackles bristling. Blackthorn uttered a low growl from deep within his throat and sank into a near crouch ready to attack. D'Arcy watched the skirmish that followed with thumping heart but it turned out to be noisy rather than bloody, with much baring of fangs, snarling and snapping and churning up of snow with muzzle biting hard enough to extract a yelp rather than blood. Blackthorn brought his opponent down and held him there. The Beta's hind leg was raised in submission and it was all over. Blackthorn stood proud and four-square in front of Granite then turned and loped off into the forest. D'Arcy waited until Granite led his pack away, then returned to the safety of the grotto.

Twilight, the time he missed Alpha-She most. It was their favourite part of the day; the time for strolling around the lake just the two of them, with pipastrelle bats flitting overhead and the air resounding with owl-cry and the chatter of running water. Fleetingly he wondered about Hushwing's desertion, but she had saved his life and he should not ask for more. But he felt so alone and friendless in this bitter white world, even her eerie screech would be a familiar and therefore welcome sound. Melancholy, he watched the fading light tint the snow-covered valley floor with shades of blue and violet and drape the mountain tops in a purple mantle. They often did that walk together, he and Alpha-She and his heart ached for her now. Did she still think of him? he wondered; or had she become angered by his continued absence and put all painful thought of him aside? The intensity of the pain this caused made him want to throw back his head and howl his hurt into the night like the wolves. A disturbing urge, he realised, watching the globe of the moon rising above the mountain ridge, butter yellow and almost at the full. A time for caution not rash urges; his pelt was already beginning to change. How he wished for an end to it all and the safety and normality of life with Alpha-She. Once this was over, if he survived, he would never leave her again.

Alpha-She sat by the darkening window pane and gazed out at the deepening twilight. A tear splashed onto the back of her hand as it rested on the window cill, and was followed by another. *Where are you D'Arcy?* her heart cried and felt as though the life were being squeezed out of it. I can never be happy again, she thought, gazing out over the purple-shadowed garden. Was he lying injured somewhere and close to death, or was he already dead? It was likely, for what else would keep him from her for so long? At this fresh tears fell and a sob tore at her throat. The thought was unbearable.

Then, as she watched the orb of the moon rise above the trees and cast long shadows over the grass, a small flame of hope spurted and warmed her heart. Twilight. Their time: that mysterious hour of shape-shifting and magic, when Reality lay between this and the Otherworld. Her spirit rose to meet it, and as the moon's beams laid a path of silver across the garden and into the wood, that other, older self leapt and raced along it, on all fours and with the wind whistling in her ears and ruffling her creamy white pelt. Onto the foothills and over the fell her spirit raced, searching for her boy. She stood alone and very still on the summit, gazing out over the valley below, sniffing and tasting the air for evidence of his presence. He was there! Her boy was alive! Alive and yearning for her just as she yearned for him, and one day he would return. Silhouetted against the moon, she tilted her head and loosed a single, haunting and undulating note into the night.

D'Arcy felt the tingle of the unknowable ripple along his spine. He moved to the entrance of the grotto and pushing aside the strands of ivy, gazed out into the deepening night. Moon-dapple covered the forest floor and the air vibrated with cold. He stood very still, listening. The wolf song was brief and sweet and brought an ache of recognition to his heart. It must be Moon-song, he reflected, yet there was no answering call from her pack, and strangely it was not she who was uppermost in his thoughts. *Alpha-She!* He no longer felt so alone, and the warmth of her love enveloped him along with the haunting notes of her soul-song. She had not cast him off after all.

The hardly discernible sound of foot-pads over crisp snow brought a rush of anticipation and tinge of guilt. Moon-song! He was lonely and far from home, he justified himself, but more than this, the weight of the Quest still lay heavily on his shoulders. Alpha-She, who loved him like no other could, would see it not as disloyalty but devotion to duty and his pursuit of the Quest. The fact that he was unsure as to the nature of this made no difference; he was here in this place because he had been led, and somehow Moon-song was part of it. The truth would unfurl like a bud in the warmth of the April sun, if only he kept faith.

She dropped part of her kill before him then greeted him with gentle nudges of her nose against his face and soft nibbles along his muzzle, in the traditional way of the wolf. He nibbled her muzzle in turn, and recalled with sadness how he and Alpha-She had done this from when he was but a few days old. He told Moon-song how relieved he was at her return, and of his foray to the edge of the forest and what he had witnessed there.

"Yes, that was Granite and Blackthorn," she said nodding solemnly. "The Alpha-Males of the old and new packs. And you were right in thinking Blackthorn is wanting to mate with a second female to swell the numbers." Here she gave him an odd look then looked away and shifted her body slightly as though uncomfortable with the situation.

"You. He wants you," D'Arcy said in a low, flat voice.

"Yes. But you haven't read the rest quite right; how could you without knowing the pack and its politics?" she added quickly to save his pride. "Granite was not, as you thought, hostile to Blackthorn on this account. Rather he sees it as a way to promote peace between the two packs. However, Granite has to maintain his advantage over Blackthorn and insist on submission to his greater authority, and to an outsider may appear aggressive. Blackthorn is young and ambitious and would otherwise try to take over the original pack."

"I see. And the wolf he was fighting?"

"That was Storm, our Beta member, the second in command and the one who deals with trouble and guards Granite. He is fierce and strong, but there was no serious intent. A mock challenge to warn Blackthorn he cannot take things for granted."

"And you – what do you want?"

"Why have you left your home and pack to live in the wilderness? Is that what *you* want?" she asked sharply, shifting her weight and leaning away from him slightly in order to watch his face. The blue eyes glittered in the moonlight and made him feel dizzy, that and her scent which since her last visit had noticeably increased in warmth and strength.

"Of course it isn't."

"So why are you here?"

The tension crackled between them now.

126

"You are talking duty," he said sullenly.

She made no reply, but her gaze left him in no doubt.

"Will you mate with him then?"

She gave him a look of such intensity that he thought he must have upset her with his directness.

"Eat," she commanded, pushing the fresh meat of her kill closer with her nose. "Go on!" she insisted as he ignored the food and would have persisted.

Reluctantly he ate whilst Moon-song watched.

She waited until he had rubbed the bloodstains from his mouth with one paw and slaked his thirst by cracking the ice on the beck outside.

"How much do you know D'Arcy, about Grey Pelt? – and the reason you are here?" she asked one they were settled again in the grotto.

He dipped his head and looked away embarrassed, then responded to her gentle prompting. "I only know that I carry his mark, and that it started amongst our breed with one of my ancestors, Fenella the Second, who called upon him in time of great danger. It is one of our sacred Pack Legends. Then some-how it drew in Destiny . . ."

"Your fey sister."

"That's right, when she saved me and our Great Grandsire Ben from drowning in Merlins Mere. Destiny understands more about the nature of him than any, yet cannot appreciate the pull of the Quest. It has come between us," he added sadly, his head and shoulders drooping as though beneath an unbearable weight. Moon-song was smiling and moving her head slowly from side to side. This puzzled him, and irritated too because she failed to understand the depth of his pain at losing his sister. She gestured for him to continue and so he carried on: "Our little Fenella the Third was the next one to be chosen; she is a smaller image of her Great Aunt Fenella and is already showing the signs."

Moon-song gave him a sidelong glance of her stunning blue eyes. "And the Quest, what do you know of that?"

"Only that my coat changes and I get strange urges every full moon that are something to do with – *Grey Pelt*." Here he dropped his voice to a hoarse whisper; one did not name him lightly.

"You called upon him," she said gravely.

"Yes, the might Destiny strayed into his lair."

"So now it is time to repay your debt."

"I suppose. Only I don't know what is wanted of me. I knew one day I would have to leave and follow the signs – like Hushwing Ghost-Owl, the midnight howling and the events that led me here to . . . well . . ." he paused, too embarrassed to voice his thoughts in case he appeared foolish.

"To me?" she supplied with a smile, but a kindly one which put him at ease because it told him she understood.

"There has to be some reason behind you saving my life and keeping me fed and sheltered. Wolves and dogs don't normally mix!"

"Yet we share common beginnings."

D'Arcy stared at her in silence and open disbelief.

"No!" he denied vehemently, shaking his head in protest. "I come from a long line of pure-bred English Setters!"

"D'Arcy, the first 'dogs' were partly-domesticated wolves! They hung around men-camps for easy meat and in time forgot how to fend for themselves. They lost their sovereignty and Men used them to hunt, and to protect their homes and families in return for food and shelter. Wolf gradually became dog, and every dog today is descended from them!"

"But we are gentle creatures, full of fun and a love of humans," D'Arcy protested.

"And we are loyal, and protective, and play with our young, and are capable of tenderness just like you. We lived alongside humans for hundreds of years. Then something went wrong, the balance tipped and Man blamed us for all his ills. He hunted us out of hatred instead of need, and exterminated us from this land."

"But he has brought you back," D'Arcy said quietly and with solemn expression.

She nodded slowly. "There are those who value our strength, loyalty and intelligence and feel we have a right to our own territory. Some though will always hate us and they protest fiercely against the idea. But lessons were learnt on both sides. Wolves and Men both got greedy and forgot how to respect each other's territory and share Mother Nature's resources. I hope through coming here that hatred will turn to tolerance, and eventually, mutual respect. Now maybe you can see why it is so essential to keep peace between the two packs."

"You are wise, Moon-song," D'Arcy said humbly.

"And you are courageous D'Arcy, that is why you were chosen as a youngster."

"For what?"

"You will know soon enough. But why are you staring like that?"

"Ever since we met I've been curious about your eyes – your *mark*!"

"All of us wolves are born with blue eyes, then as we grow they change to yellow or green but mine stayed blue. It is very rare, and yes, marked me out."

"You know what I mean – is it *his mark*?"

"He comes to me at times."

"The others must have thought it weird, you having blue eyes I mean."

"They picked on me at first because I was different, so I learned to scrap good! They left me alone then."

"I bet they did!" D'Arcy exclaimed in admiration. "And now?"

"They are afraid of me. I think they would have liked to drive me out but dare not. But they also see my blue eyes as a sign of power and status for the pack."

"Do they know why?"

"Granite suspects some deeper meaning so dare not oppose me."

"And Blackthorn? Is he not afraid?"

"Probably, but he is greedy for power."

"But surely, Granite could not afford to part with you, especially to a rival pack? If you go, you take your powers with you."

"The plan is for me to be 'go-between'; the one chosen to promote tolerance, if not harmony, between the old and new packs. Granite has decided I should spend time with both. That way he holds on to his status symbol, and also achieves peace between the packs, so essential if wolves are to be allowed to remain here."

"Is it possible?"

"The two packs can hunt and inhabit their own territory; this valley is big enough for that. As for me, Blackthorn fears what he sees as my power and also knows he is no match for Granite and his pack, so will accept his terms."

"There is so much that I didn't know! But I still don't know why I was brought here."

"And now I must go."

D'Arcy's heart sank as he watched her leave. English Setters, he told himself, are not meant to live alone. Without the company of human or four-foot they slip into a decline, so little wonder he was desolate at her departure. Heaving a huge sigh he settled down, curled around and tucked tail over nose ready for sleep.

Minutes later he was back on his feet, alert and standing at the entrance. His ears trawled for the sound that had awakened him, and nose tested the air for warning scents. There it was again, the scuffle, grunts and growls of a struggle between two animals, followed by a high-pitched squeal that sent him crashing through the ivy curtain and racing into the darkness.

Wolf Spirit

15.

D'Arcy Wolf-Shadow: Grey Pelt keeps the covenant

Following scent, sound and paw prints, he hurtled into a clearing in the forest.

"Moon-song!"

At the intensity of his cry, the brittle air splintered and branches shuddered and shed crystals of snow. By the cold light of the almost full moon two wolves were locked in confrontation. The male, whom he instantly recognised as Blackthorn, had forepaws hooked around her neck and was attempting to mount her back. Moon-song was threshing about in an attempt to dislodge him whilst turning her head, mouth open and ready to snap.

"Are you so crass you don't know I'm not ready yet!" she snarled.

Intent on business Blackthorn seemed unaware of her words or D'Arcy's presence, or afforded it little significance. Shocked and afraid, D'Arcy froze. The churning of bodies in snow, snarling and growling were terrifying and alien to a gentle Setter soul. Blackthorn grunted as Moon-song's head whipped round and she managed to nip his shoulder. A high-pitched squeal from Moon-song as the male sank his teeth into her neck broke D'Arcy's trance and sent him flying across the moonlit clearing.

"Get off her!" he barked fiercely, swinging his rear round to buffet Blackthorn's flank in warning.

"Go eat dung, human-lover!" Blackthorn snarled, turning his head and baring his fangs.

D'Arcy inwardly quaked, but refused to back off. The sight of Moon-song's foam-flecked muzzle and staring eyes, coupled with her yelps and cries of pain, pushed him beyond the limit.

"Leave her alone, wolf-dung!" he shouted, swinging his rear yet again to deliver a punishing blow which, coupled with slippery snow underfoot, served to throw the male wolf off-balance.

"I'll kill you, runt, when I've finished here!" he panted, renewing his efforts to ride Moon-song's back.

"You've finished!" D'Arcy snarled, biting Blackthorn's hind leg in the soft muscle above the hock.

Yelping with pain and surprise Buckthorn lost both his footing and his hold on Moon-song. He whipped round and baring his fangs in a formidable snarl, launched himself at D'Arcy who fell beneath the impact. He screamed at the searing pain in his shoulder as Blackthorn sank his teeth into the tender flesh. The sheer weight and bulk of the wolf's body threatened to crush the life from his fragile by comparison frame. Vaguely D'Arcy was aware of a ring of faces watching from between the trees at the edge of the clearing. The air was split with snarling, growling and Moon-song's curses but above it all rose a fearful screech. D'Arcy did not hear it; Blackthorn's head was hooked over his neck and pressing down, down, down to make him submit. Foam-flecked, bleeding and exhausted from kicking, biting and using his Setter speed to manoeuvre his body out of range of flashing fangs, he knew he was close to the end. In a last effort D'Arcy bucked and managed to throw him off and they locked in deadly combat. The two bodies rolled and threshed in the snow then were still. Blackthorn had brought him down and was standing astride in triumph. D'Arcy lay in the bloodstained snow, panting and fighting for the next breath.

"Spare him? Spare him you say? Not likely, this human-loving, dung-heap of a dog attacked an Alpha wolf and must die!" Blackthorn was howling.

D'Arcy waited for the death-blow.

A fearful shriek sounded above Moon-song's curses and threats aimed at Blackthorn in an attempt to secure D'Arcy's release. This time D'Arcy heard it, and turning his head a fraction saw a white ghostly shape sail low overhead. *Hushwing!* Was she about to save him again? Yet even as the thought raced through his mind, he knew that this time her intervention would not be allowed.

> *When Hushwing flies and bats are at play*
> *Grey Pelt is never far away!*

Unbidden, those lines from Destiny's song echoed inside his head. At least I have died defending your Quest, he thought, gasping what felt to be his last breath. *Maybe Grey Pelt will ease my passing.* He thought he must be dying as his limbs stiffened and stretched and his neck arched in a painful spasm. Moon-song's howls of sorrow reached him through the fug of pain and resignation, as she came to the same conclusion. A small flame of fury spurted that she should be caused such distress and fuelled a passion for revenge. This seemed to replenish his strength, which rather than deserting him was returning fourfold. His muscles bunched and flexed with power, and his lips curled back to make room for elongated teeth revealed in a fearsome snarl. He gasped and the world went dark as an awesome power entered his body.

A black cloud of energy crept from hindquarters to head, taking over his body and mind. Quick as the flick of a lizard's tongue his muscles bunched, seemingly of their own accord, and he leapt to his feet flinging the unwary Blackthorn aside. Loosing a terrible spine-chilling growl he crouched and sprang. It was over before Hushwing's scream of triumph had died on the shivering air. Buckthorn squealed in terror and prostrated himself on the snow in total submission.

D'Arcy stood above him, threw back his head and howled his triumph at the moon.

Blackthorn crept away in shame, and the pack members who had heard the battle and gathered to watch, one by one melted into the night. All except Granite and Storm, who stood motionless at the edge of the forest. Storm hung back a few paces, guarding his Alpha's rear. Granite met and held Moon-song's gaze for a long moment and D'Arcy felt the flow of communication between them, but was not privy to its content. Finally, sensing some hidden power within D'Arcy, Granite dipped his head in respect then turned and loped away with Storm at his heels, and was soon swallowed up by the forest.

"You are making a habit of this," Moon-song murmured in between licking his wounds clean inside the den. She made no mention of the sudden transformation that she must know to be the work of Grey Pelt, and for this D'Arcy was grateful. When alone, he would mull it over and no doubt be filled with fresh awe and gratitude, but right now he wanted the illusion of normality and pretence that it had not taken place.

D'Arcy winced and grunted. "Your tongue's as rough as a sheep's bum!"

"Now how would you know that?" she teased, pausing in her licking. "But you have no infection in your leg now, do you?"

"None."

"Then lie still and don't grumble," she scolded with mock severity, licking with renewed vigour.

"I'm grateful Moon-song, you'll never know how much."

"Silly boy." But there was a softness in her voice that made him wonder. He could not help noticing that her scent was strong to the point of overpowering and exciting him despite his pain and exhaustion. Had she meant that taunt to the inexperienced Blackthorn about not being ready? Or was it a ploy to avoid mating with him? His heart raced; he too was inexperienced, and so did not know the answer and was embarrassed by his naivety.

"There, you'll do," she said at last, giving his flank one final lick. "Sleep now, and I'll come tomorrow."

"Can you not stay?" he pleaded, reaching out to touch her with his forepaw.

His maleness would not allow him to betray the depth of his despair at her leaving, but there must have been a flavour of it in his touch.

"D'Arcy, you must not come to depend on me." She touched his paw in return to soften her words. "You must know we cannot be together," she added, and given the pain in those blue eyes it was as though she had added *even though I want it too.*

"Why? Why couldn't we?" A momentary but profound silence fell; he had dared to voice the forbidden. "I don't believe we met by accident; it was meant," he continued, knowing there could be no going back.

"Yes, we were destined to meet," she agreed, and he sensed a sadness as deep as his own. "But because of the Quest, and that must be enough. You must keep faith D'Arcy, that it will all come right one day, and that any distress now will then be worthwhile."

Seeing the pain etched in her face and feeling the waves of sadness gave him the courage to voice what he now knew. "You feel the same, Moon-song."

"We would be hunted throughout our lives and eventually killed, either by one or both packs, or Man."

"It would be better than being alone," he declared stoutly.

She gave him a long look and a sad little smile. "You are a brave boy D'Arcy, and pure at heart."

"You think I'm just a dreamer! But we could defy them all," he urged, desperate now as he watched her move to the mouth of the cave.

"Maybe," she said gravely, "but only if you are prepared to leave your home and family for ever."

With this she disappeared leaving behind an unbearable loneliness. Her words echoed around the emptiness of the cave, mocking his bravado and filling his heart and mind with despair.

That night was the darkest and bleakest of D'Arcy's life. He passed it in fitful sleep between long hours of misery and mounting despair. In order to survive he would have to forage for food, an exercise already marked by abject failure, or return home with tail between legs. Yet even if he could make it over the snow and ice-clad mountain, and this was unlikely given his weakened state and lack of food for the journey, how could he face Alpha-She and the pack? He had failed miserably in his pursuit of the Quest, and had nothing but scars and a matted coat and wasted body to show for his period of desertion. To have left them knowing Joey to be ill, and be absent at his passing, was surely unforgivable, and how much more so when he could not return with pride in his success, but was forced to crawl back in disgrace. No, it was better to perish here alone with his shame.

Despite the inexorable passage of time, Alpha-She had not given up on her boy; she still roamed the fells each day calling his name and searching all his old haunts. Neither had Destiny it seemed. She often went missing for a day and came back dishevelled and weary. Alpha-She tried to stop her at first, watching her every moment and calling out sharply whenever Destiny started sloping off up the fell on her own. After a while though she gave up the struggle and was heard telling Alpha-He that if it helped her to feel she was doing something to find her brother, then she knew what that feeling was like and wouldn't stand in her way. Besides Destiny always managed to slip away and find an escape route no matter how closely watched. So Alpha-She grew gaunter and Destiny, always a plump little bitch, grew thinner and both wore grief draped around them in an isolating veil.

One frosty morning after Destiny had arrived home exhausted the night before, the two little girls approached Tickle. "I'm worried about Destiny," Flossie said, her dark eyes brimming with anxiety.

"So am I," Fenella said at her rear. "But I've told Flossie, we have to trust her; she knows things we don't."

"But she is so thin and doesn't connect with us any more. It's bad enough losing one of the Twins, but to lose both of them would be unbearable," wailed Flossie, giving way to her distress. "I'm scared she will be too weak to make it home one day, or even die if this goes on any longer."

"Now, now dear, don't distress yourself . . ." Tickle started to say but was stopped in mid-sentence.

"Destiny will not die," Fenella intervened in a strange flat sort of voice.

Flossie turned and stared at her sister and Tickle's nose twitched as though scenting something odd but not unfamiliar.

"How do you know, Fenella?" Tickle prompted.

Fenella's eyes glazed over and she appeared to be gazing at a point beyond them and seemed unaware of their presence. Tickle and Flossie exchanged looks and nodded. They had seen that far-away look many times on Destiny's face, especially when she got one of her feelings that something was about to happen, or when a song was coming on.

"What do you know Fenella?" Tickle demanded, pumping her paw up and down in her impatience to hear any scrap of news about her beloved Twins.

"Last night I saw Destiny and D'Arcy in a dream. Destiny was watching from afar, but is keeping faith with him, and so has protection and strength beyond her self."

Fenella's voice trailed away but she continued to stare with that strange out-of-it-all expression.

"And D'Arcy, what of him?" Tickle pressed, her face creased with anxiety.

"In the dream I saw a great Shadow-wolf in a midnight sky," Fenella continued in that odd monotone so unlike her normal voice. "I could see the stars shining around but also through him, and way below was the tiny dark figure of D'Arcy on a vast snow-covered plain. He was so weak and frail and lost that he could not see beyond the snow-drifts, or fight the dangers that threatened. He was close to giving up."

"Oh, my poor boy!" Tickle whispered and her face crumpled in distress.

"The Shadow-wolf loomed over D'Arcy," Fenella continued, seemingly unaware of the interruption, "and breathed out a cloud of Wolf-power, a sort of dark energy, if you like. It billowed down to the ground and over D'Arcy then disappeared. I think it went inside him because his tiny figure grew and grew and looked more like the wolf in the sky than himself. He seemed stronger than ever before, and was able to fight and defeat his enemy, and overcome any obstacles in his way."

"And is he coming home?" Tickle asked urgently, her paw thumping up and down in her excitement. Her tone seemed to jerk Fenella out of her reverie. She blinked rapidly and the far-off look left her face. She gazed at Tickle

"I—, I don't know Tickle. I don't quite understand . . ." she petered off and looked bewildered as though awaking from a deep sleep.

"It's all right Fenella," Tickle soothed. "You are safe. We can take some comfort from what you have told us, can't we Flossie?"

"It was just a dream." Fenella looked anxious as though fearing the pack may expect too much.

"Now what has Destiny told you?" Tickle said sternly.

"Well, I—"

"She says there's no such thing as 'just' a dream," Flossie, seeing her little sister's embarrassment, answered for her "at least, not where you two are concerned, and not when it's about something so significant. It is guidance from our helpers in the Otherworld. They send us pictures because that is easiest for us to understand." Flossie, suddenly realising that she had become the focus of awed attention and was sounding much too authoritative for her years and no-nonsense nature, went pink around the gills. "Anyway," she mumbled, passing it off by pretending to scratch her ear with one forepaw, "that's what Destiny says."

"Flossie is right," Tickle said, patting Flossie's paw reassuringly. "You have your Aunt Destiny's gift, Fenella – and we all know she is for real!" she finished, and comforted the littlest one with a quick lick to the ear.

"Should we tell the others? It might help them too, even Destiny," Flossie added, confidence and poise restored.

"I think so. Follow me girls!" Tickle stomped her way importantly into the kitchen with Flossie and Fenella trailing behind. The youngsters whispered as they went, agreeing that it was wonderful to have their strong and capable Nan Tickle back with them again.

Tickle took the floor and gravely told the others that she had 'something of importance to impart', then when she had their attention, introduced Fenella and directed her to tell them all about her experience of the previous night. Faltering at first and patently nervous, Fenella related the facts simply and in her normal voice. Even so the silence that followed betrayed the impact of this revelation. Clifford unexpectedly was first to sit up and speak.

"Well done, Little One, you have brought us some hope," he said solemnly, much in the way that Joey might have done. The others stared at him in stunned surprise. Clifford's eye's widened and his left ear stuck out at right angles so that he resembled a rabbit startled by its own audacity. He sank down into a corner of the settle and tried to look inconspicuous.

Pippa, fond of Clifford since that first welcome, nodded and stepped into the gap. "I agree, Clifford. Personally, I don't really understand all this Otherworld stuff, but I'm more hopeful of D'Arcy's return, now I know Destiny is in there helping him in some way."

"What do you think, Destiny?" Flossie probed craftily, "did Fenella get it right? Does part of you know somehow that your brother is still alive"

"Fenella related the bones of her experience 'as it was' – so you don't need me to confirm it. It is for you to give it meaning," Destiny replied, neatly avoiding a direct confirmation, whilst leaving them all with the distinct impression of having given exactly that.

"When will he return, Destiny?' Clifford asked, sitting up straight again. The others looked at him and speculated: was he finding his role of acting leader too onerous, or secretly wanting D'Arcy to stay away in order to hold on to it for good? Given his uncharacteristic taking of the lead just now, there could be some grounds for suspicion on that last count. Destiny shook her head so slightly that the movement was almost imperceptible, but her upright stance and raised tail left them in no doubt of her disapproval. Shamefaced, they lowered their heads slightly for having even for a moment entertained such an uncharitable thought, and each member secretly wondered how it could have come about.

"When he has completed the Quest, Clifford. And you are doing a super job of standing in for him," Destiny added warmly, so that Clifford's muzzle turned pink and both ears stuck out with pleasure. She turned a sterner look on the others, "Until then we must all play our part by sticking together," she told them all. "It's a dangerous time for us, with all this uncertainty and distress. Unless we believe in each other no matter what, we'll lose our way and the Pack will falter and fail," she added grimly.

"We're up for it Destiny!" the others chorused, and the pack went to bed that night happier than they had done since the night of D'Arcy's disappearance.

However, alone in his dark and cold cave, a million miles from the warmth and comfort of both home and pack, D'Arcy listened to the strains of a wolf howl drifting through the night. Tonight more haunting than ever, it seemed to be Moon-song's poignant and final farewell. As the last note faded and he lay there alone, he wondered miserably how long it would take to die of hunger.

Moonrise and Mystery

16.

Winter Solstice

It seemed starvation was a redundant fear, at least for the time being. He awoke to the reflected light from a fresh snowfall filtering in through the ivy – and a skinned rabbit lying outside. His heart leapt with gratitude at what he took to be Moon-song's final kindly act. Ravenous appetite appeased, his thoughts took a slightly more optimistic turn: from the outset of this strange adventure each move had been cloaked in uncertainty. Life was a book of mysteries, and one never knew what would appear on the next page. Just as the rabbit was unexpected bounty, something may yet turn up to save him.

An optimism that waned as the coldness and loneliness of the day wore on. By the time the streaks of greenish light and mauve twilight had faded from the sky, and the snow was overlaid with deep troughs of purple shadow, despair came creeping in again.

He had tried his luck at stalking and catching prey, but all he had to show for his pains were a couple of blackbird feathers clutched from the tail of the intended victim as, flapping and chattering angrily, it fled into the bushes. On top of everything, the weather had taken a turn for the worse. Snow showers had dogged him throughout the day, covering up tracks and making the prospect of a successful hunt even more absurd. Now the sky was heavy with menace; stormy cumuli were riding in on the back of a bitter north westerly wind. Cold, lonely, aching from his fresh wounds and thoroughly disheartened he crept back into the cave.

He was convinced that Moon-song would never again return, so her sudden appearance at the entrance with the moon silvering her pelt, and the joy that sprang up within at sight of her, made him blink rapidly and wonder if he was in the midst of a wonderful dream. She approached and laid before him some withered-looking leaves and berries, then touched his nose in greeting.

"I thought you had left for good," he murmured, nibbling her muzzle in greeting.

If he sensed the significance behind her failure to reply, he chose to ignore it. For now he was relieved and overjoyed at not having to spend the night alone.

"The Lady Moon is at the full tonight – and it is also the Winter Solstice," she murmured. "A special, magical night. You should not have to spend it alone."

He stared steadily at her, searching for a clue to her mood and intent. Tonight she disturbed him, was too enigmatic for him to understand. She had about her the air of strangeness, of an inhabitant of the Otherworld cloaked in mystery and wisdom, yet the ethereal was contradicted by a marked increase in the heady, musky scent that was undisputedly physical, and which rose from her body whenever she moved. It stirred his maleness and intoxicated his senses.

"What exactly is the Winter Solstice?" he asked, ashamed of his ignorance.

"The Longest Night. And the magical time each year when Earth tilts furthest away from the sun."

"But that is not a good thing surely?"

"Oh but it is, because it marks the turning point. From tomorrow each day will be a tiny bit longer, the nights shorter. The darkness and silence of this time is the secret cosmic womb from which the Sun will be reborn. We must celebrate future new life, D'Arcy."

A silence fell between them and D'Arcy wondered at the intensity of the look she gave him. Whatever it conveyed could not be. Her scent was driving him beyond the barriers of prohibition, but the thought alone was an aberration, a profanity of Nature. He quickly thought of something, anything, to say to break through the barrier of that disturbing silence.

"So, it is a special time then."

"Yes, but even more so tonight, because the moon is at the full, increasing the magic and power of the Solstice. Now eat," she said, indicating the leaves and berries.

"What are they?" he frowned and looked at them without appetite.

"Dried herbs, and berries. They have powerful healing properties to ease your pain and disquiet."

"I don't need them now you are here."

The blue eyes seemed to glow in the semi-dark, compelling him to obey. She moved to the exit, gave him an enigmatic look and raised a paw when he would have protested. "Things are not always what they seem. Trust me, D'Arcy."

Then she was gone.

He was bereft. He lay there in the dark, head on the ground and with pain in his heart. She had given by coming when he had not expected it, then taken away his happiness by leaving again, thus making the pain keener and more heartfelt than if she had not come at all. He looked distastefully at the bundle of unappetising leaves and berries at his feet. This then was her way of easing her farewell. Yet something in those blue eyes had penetrated self pity and left a reasonable doubt. *Trust me!* After all she had done for him, was that not the least he could do? Whatever, if these herbs and berries could ease his pain and her guilt at leaving him, then what had he got to lose? He heaved a sigh of resignation and began to eat.

Before long his head began to buzz and his body felt lighter and lighter as though he could rise above it and leave it behind on the floor of the grotto. It was not an unpleasant feeling and instead of resisting as he initially had, he drifted along with it. Strange lights flashed and blinked behind his eyes, then when he blinked them out of his head they floated around inside the walls of the grotto. One, larger and brighter than the others and glowing with subtle shades of gold tinted with greens and blues, drifted slowly but purposefully towards the exit, hovered a moment, then disappeared only to reappear and float away again. Compelled to follow, D'Arcy rose from his bed of dried leaves and heather and moving to the entrance, pushed aside the over-hanging growth allowing the moonlight to stream inside. He turned then and felt momentarily puzzled, yet strangely no sense of fear or shock, at the sight of the still form on the bed. Then he was through the opening and gone.

He was big and strong and loped through the moonlit night with ease. His muscles bulged beneath the skin and his limbs were elongated and driving him forward with unaccustomed power; and the dark streak that ran the length of his back bristled and lifted in the wind as his huge pads sped over the snow. He ran on compelled by a force beyond his understanding, pausing for less than the blink of an owl's eye to look overhead as a piercing screech split the sky. Hushwing Ghost-Owl glided on the westerly wind and from time to time turned her head, compelling him onward with a glare from the great yellow lamps of her eyes. Whenever crossed paths or uncertainty momentarily slackened his pace, Hushwing swooped and hovered ahead and urged him on with unearthly shrieks. On he raced through the snow-covered forest to emerge onto the moon-drenched plain of the dalehead, the place where he had confronted and beaten Blackthorn. *The place of your strength, because here you found your true self* a voice within seemed to say. He slowed and came to a halt and stood looking around the empty clearing. By day just that, but now silent, snow-hushed and silvered by moonlight it was a ghostly and magical space. As though triggered by this revelation, a haunting cry wavered on the ice-brittle air, then gathering strength, rose and billowed into the night as a paean to Lady Moon and a call to the secret wolf within. He followed the sound to the snow-capped summit and the sight that met his gaze strangled the breath in his throat. She stood silhouetted against the full moon, head back and giving voice to her wildness and nobility. For it was she; he would recognise that graceful line and slightness of build anywhere. And she was calling him to her; this he knew now for sure.

He could no more resist that call than stop breathing. He leapt, bound and threaded his way to the mountain top and confronted her there. The last haunting note of her song died away and she turned to face him. Her eyes in the moonlight glowed ice-blue and were slanted and partially hooded in silent invitation. The scent of her was so strong and heady it made his senses swim and excitement soar to unbearable heights. She turned then and presented to him. There was only a second's hesitation, not out of any sense of honour about to be betrayed as he felt only the rightness of this act to which they had both been inexorably led, but rather a momentary fear of inadequacy. Then awareness of his new strength and vigour, of his lineage and place in the Shadow World they shared, overcame any such reservation.

The winter-storm that had been gathering all day rumbled above their heads and finally broke. As he moved to the age-old rhythm thunder roared and lighting flashed, the strobe-lights holding for seconds the now immobile pair on the mountain top as they waited for culmination and history to be forged. When finally they parted, he threw back his head and for the second time during his time at Weirdale, howled his triumph into the night. The ancient undulating notes of his anthem were swelled by those of Moon-song. She loosed her hopes of fruitfulness and sent them soaring skyward, beseeching the Moon Goddess to smile upon them and grant them success in their endeavour.

Then, unbelievably, their joint song was overlaid by another, stronger and altogether more plaintive one, so pure and poignant it had to have its roots in the Otherworld. Awestruck, they stood in silence to listen. D'Arcy gazed across the valley to the opposite peak. He stood silhouetted against the moon, the great primordial beast that had commandeered his life and brought him to this place.

"Grey Pelt," he whispered and bowed his head in homage.

With Moon-song by his side, D'Arcy watched the Spirit of the Last Wolf of Lakeland fade into the swirling storm clouds.

Their parting was tender and poignant, but he re-entered the grotto filled with a new warmth and confidence and a pride in an act well executed. He had fulfilled his Quest. What consequences would follow nobody knew, but he had to believe in the rightness of what had taken place. In any case, his head was too thick and fuzzy for ponderous thoughts, and he was staggering about like the birds and the deer in the orchard when they had gorged on fermenting fruit. He collapsed onto his heather bed, and on the slight shock of impact was confused about whether he had actually travelled in his body or whether something beyond the physical had taken place. Yet his feet were cold and damp, his chest feathers wet from the depth of snow in the drifts. Unable to fathom the mystery, he put aside unanswerable questions and slipped into the deep and dreamless slumber of the exhausted.

When he awoke at dawn it took a while for the memory to take shape in his mind, the response to his probing coming together bit by bit like the words in Alpha-She's crossword puzzles. The images flashed through his mind, at once beguiling and frustrating as they slipped away again before he could grasp and imprison them in memory: the glint of moonlight on snow, the peaks that slumbered in midnight shadow shuddering into life beneath the crackle and streak of lightning; a small but proud silhouette against the moon; her blue eyes glowing with invitation; then remembered oneness and ecstasy; and finally Grey Pelt honouring their union with his presence. Had it really happened? Would there be issue? And if so, what would happen to creatures born between two worlds and two different species? And would Moon-song visit him still? The answers to the first questions were beyond him, but he knew with great sadness that Moon-song would not return; their parting had an air of finality about it. There still remained the question of his survival and need of food but if, as he suspected, he had played his part in the cosmic game, maybe he was dispensable. He could bear even that, he thought, if only he could be spared long enough to know the truth.

17.

Time Warp: D'Arcy wanders alone and confused in the wilderness

Day followed on dreary day, tedious despite the thaw which set the beck running free and the surface of the pool, until now prisoner beneath a skin of ice, reflecting a high and windswept sky that brought to mind the blue of Moon-song's eyes. Water he had in plenty then, and somehow he managed to survive with some unexpected help. Initially, however, his concern was not for his bodily needs but for the companionship and support that he had come to rely upon and which was necessary to his well-being. He roamed the valley in search of Moon-song but without success. The space was vast, the woods and forests dark and deep and along with the crags and gullies, offered too many places to hide. It was ideal territory for a being not wishing to be found, and he had to accept now that, for whatever reason, Moon-song was just that. It was not that he wanted to stay with her for ever. No, following that fateful night this desire had abated, as though in the culmination of their liaison he had been released from some strange enchantment and now longed only for home and the life he had left behind. Rather he sought her companionship, and the comfort of a friendly being to inhabit his lonely world – if only for a few brief moments each day.

A genuine fondness had developed too, and with it concern for her welfare, and her status with the rival packs. Had both Granite and Blackthorn disowned her and driven her out to fend alone? If so, how was she faring? Above all, he wished to discover the truth of her condition, to know if what he still saw as his betrayal of his own clan had been justified and worthwhile. If so, he needed to ensure that Moon-song had sufficient food and support for her needs, and to let her know he would stand by her, no matter what. Yet he felt somehow redundant, as though his part in the drama had been played and he was no longer needed. Far from bringing a sense of relief this filled him with hurt and frustration. He still had little understanding of why the event was brought about or what Grey Pelt hoped to achieve for the wolves, but sensed it to be of great significance. And he missed her; he missed her no-nonsense warmth, her practical capabilities combined with Mother-wisdom and awareness of the Quest. She was marked just as he was, and was as much a puppet in the cosmic game. The differences were superficial; in essence they were the same.

Each night he returned to the grotto and lay alone and friendless on his bed. He would sleep then from sheer exhaustion and find solace in dreams of home, his Pack and Alpha-She. In those dreams he would be running with them on the mountain side, or chasing the little girls around Merlins Mere. He grew thinner and gaunter, his coat and feathering became tangled and bedraggled and was home to burrs, twigs and sprigs of prickly gorse. Isolation – always alien and intolerable to a Setter – began to take its toll. His mind wandered from time to time and he lost track of where he was and his purpose in being there.

As to his survival, that was ensured in a totally unexpected way. A couple of days after the Solstice whilst out searching for Moon-song, he had seen the figure of a man emerge from the forest. He had watched for a moment, drawn by the sight of another living being to stay longer than he should before running away, so that the man had caught sight of him, called out in a friendly way then given chase, but without real hope of catching his quarry. Later that day curiosity, and a ravening hunger sharpened by the smell of fresh meat, had driven him to approach the area again but with extreme caution. He found a hunk of meat had been left at the edge of the glade. It carried the scent of the man, and D'Arcy knew he had left it for him. The pattern was repeated on subsequent days and D'Arcy, starved not just of food but communion with another living being, allowed him to draw a little closer. The man spoke to him in soft tones and had the stance and smell and aura of a human com-passionate to animals.

"What you doin' out here all alone, a fine fella like you?" he said in soft tones that soothed D'Arcy's loneliness, then added: "Where is she? Has she left you all alone to fend for yourself, mate?"

D'Arcy stared at the man and wondered how he could possibly know about Moon-song. Was he part of it all too, of the tangled web of connections that made up the Quest? Surely not? This was not a man-thing, yet how had he come by that knowledge, unless he had seen them together, which was unlikely.

It seemed there was no logical answer.

The man also carried the scent of wolf. D'Arcy's nostrils twitched as they picked up the smell of Granite and Blackthorn – the strongest scents of the strongest males, and then a blend of lesser males and females too similar to stand alone. He sifted the air in vain for Moon-song's scent; either she was not now a member of either pack or was no longer alive. He pushed away the latter as too painful to contemplate. True, if they suspected her of fraternising with an outsider, the packs could have turned on her, as in the ordinary way they would, but her blue eyes and healing skills made her special – and they were frightened of her, and with luck too afraid to risk driving her off or taking her life. He had to fervently hope this was the case. It may even be that Granite was aware of hidden things too and was part of the plan, and had placed her beneath his protection. From these scents D'Arcy knew then that this was one of the men who monitored the packs and provided extra kill in winter, as told to him by Moon-song. Every few days a joint of meat would be left for him, in the same place and time. It offered some sort of security; he grew to rely upon it, and on the presence of the man. But D'Arcy never let him get close enough to touch.

Then came what could have been a turning point in D'Arcy's life. He had spent a miserable and sleepless night when loneliness had pressed in from all sides and his world felt empty and life not worthwhile. Because of this, the following morning he welcomed the man's presence and allowed to draw closer than ever before.

"Still on your own lad? You're obviously lost and if someone was going to claim you, well they would have done so by now. Wanna come home with me then?" the man said easily, slowly extending one hand and holding it out, still and steady and making no move to touch him. For one second D'Arcy was tempted to let this man into his life, to go with him purely to end his loneliness, fear and isolation. Instinctively he knew this tall rangy man in his green and tan forester clothes would care for him and keep him safe. But then in that instant of wavering, Alpha-She flashed into his mind and he knew he could not do it. Either he would die here alone or one day be allowed to return but he did not belong with anyone else, however kind.

"Okay boy," the man said withdrawing his hand. "But if you change your mind I'm sure you'll let me know. Meantime, I can at least keep you going in rations! But better watch those wolves don't get you!" he added.

If only he knew! D'Arcy thought, but took the warning as it was meant, with compassion and concern for his welfare.

Time passed and he found himself thinking *if it had really happened she would be whelping about now.* Yet still there had been no sign of her, either alone or in the glimpses he caught of the two packs until finally he gave up hope. It never happened; it must have been a sort of waking-dream brought on by those leaves and berries, he told himself. Sick at heart and lonely for Destiny, the Alpha-Pair and of course the Pack (he no longer referred to it in his thoughts as 'my' pack believing he had forfeited that right) he longed to go home but his pride would not permit him to return as a miserable failure. Neither was he sure of a welcome. Better by far to eke out his time here in ignorance of that fact, than to be faced with being shunned and turned away by those he loved, because that would break his heart.

The Silver Pelt

18.

Betwixt Two Worlds

Sleepless and swamped by sadness, D'Arcy gazed at his reflection in the pool close to the grotto and struggled with an overwhelming sense of shame. How foolish to have believed it could ever actually have happened. It was not real. It was a figment of his imagination and wishful thinking. Now he had to die here alone or return to the Pack as a failure and hope that they would accept him back as their Top Dog. But why should they? He had not been there for them. During their time of greatest need he had been off chasing phantoms whilst their Top Dog lay dying. And he didn't even have the excuse of success to justify his absence and claim it to be worthwhile. He did not deserve to be forgiven. A misery as dark and heavy as thunder clouds draped itself around his shoulders. As he stared at his reflection with something close to loathing a gust of wind ruffled the water's surface, shattering his image and startling him with the suddenness of movement. It chilled the back of his neck causing his hackles to rise so that he whipped round, alert despite his sorrow.

She was standing in the clearing, the areas of white on her pelt transmuted to silver by the shaft of moonlight streaming down through the treetops. Immature but neat and perfectly formed, she was a magical thing from another world. The sheer wonder of that sight stole his breath away and waves of shock zigzagged through his belly to his spine and down to his loins. Beguilement warred with age-old fear and the need to flee. His acceptance by her kind would be unknown to this stranger, therefore making him vulnerable to attack. She was not a member of Granite's Pack, or Blackthorn's either: such beauty would have stood out amongst its members and he did not recognise this female.

That isn't true! an inner voice whispered. He tried hard to ignore it, yet despite himself something deep in his belly was stirring, a primeval source of recognition that lay beyond the logic and common sense of this world. It could not be; she was unreal – a creature of the Otherworld and fear pierced his heart. But then he noticed the mud-speckled thighs and the rhythmical heaving of flank. She had the appearance of one who had travelled far over solid fell and forested land. Was that what he had recognised, a fellow seeker on an impossible quest?

You are running from the truth, the inner voice taunted.
The almond-shaped eyes watched him with unblinking stare.
Was it possible? He looked her over more critically, noting her youthfulness – the strong limbs muscled and sinewy but still with much growing to do, and the sheen of softness on a pelt not yet coarsened by adulthood. His stomach lurched at the realisation that she was scarcely more than a cub. It was just possible. She moved sideways as though to turn and retreat, and it was then that he saw them, the streaks and flecks of bluish-black threading the silver pelt. There was no flight, no move to retreat into the wood and he realised with a jolt that she had stood thus on purpose to display her markings. D'Arcy's heart lurched in his

chest as she turned. She also bore a dark streak running from eye to ear. *His* streak. *The Silver Pelt.*

He was never to be sure whether he whispered those words aloud or whether she read his mind. She turned slowly in the moonlight to face him again and moved toward him with slowness and deliberation. Her eyes became slanted and she looked away then back again to show her lack of hostility, then looked directly at him, and he felt the shock of emotion as they connected. A shaft of moonlight slanting across her head revealed almond-shaped, translucent eyes of a familiar shade of blue. He felt as though his legs would give way, were too weak with shock to hold him. She blinked in an age-old gesture of acknowledgement and he knew for sure that she recognised him too. Later he would silently rail at himself for not speaking, for not moving to her side to ask at least some of the questions that burned his mind; during that few moments of enchantment he could do nothing but stand and stare. Yet later again he would realise the impropriety and forbidden aspect of attempting anything more.

For all her youth she bore herself with dignity and D'Arcy's heart felt as though it might burst with pride. A momentary sadness gripped it as he sensed her intention to leave. She raised her head then slowly dipped it in acknowledgement and homage before melting into the moon-soaked mist.

He stared into the dark, moon-shot space that had held her, and his soul sang.

"I did it Joey," he whispered. "Thanks to you, I completed my Quest."

He turned back to the pool and stared down at his reflection and it seemed he had grown, that his chest was broader, his head more noble and his coat shone silver in the reflected light from the moon.

He started and his heart thumped against his ribs as a shadow appeared at his side and a second reflection – a mirror-image of his own – appeared in the pool.

"Destiny!"

He whipped round to face her and was overcome with emotion.

"Are you coming home now bro, or what?"

"You haven't changed, sis!"

"You have."

It was simply stated, and he had no way of knowing how much or little she had witnessed but as their eyes met, he knew she was aware that something momentous had taken place.

"I thought never to see you again," he whispered, his voice choked with emotion.

"No such luck!" she quipped, but added gravely, "I had not thought you would be away so long."

"Neither did I. If I had known, I doubt I would have left." His eyes searched her face for signs of censure or forgiveness.

"Then it's a good thing you didn't know; there was a Quest to accomplish!"

Faced with her graciousness and understanding, D'Arcy was almost undone. He licked her eyes and muzzle with infinite tenderness.

His eyes filled with compassion on seeing her bloody paws from the journey over the mountain, and he made her lie down and spent several minutes in licking them clean.

"You suffered this for me," he said humbly, licking her pads clean of blood.

"Somebody had to keep an eye on you," she said brusquely, but brother-love shone from eyes that but for the colour, in their depth and luminosity held a disturbing resemblance to those of Moon-song, a fact he had noticed before but failed to register.

"But how did you find me?"

"Your ancestors are mine too remember," she answered as though having read his mind. She flexed one paw experimentally, and her eyes teased him as she added. "I tracked you. I would know your scent anywhere."

"The Alpha-Pair must be demented at both of us going AWOL."

"I haven't been staying away as long as you! At first Alpha-She was devastated when I went missing overnight, then she began to sense I was helping you and had to be left to do it in my own way. She realised I would always return."

D'Arcy looked puzzled. "But the scent-trail must have gone cold."

"Maybe, but you were always clumsy! Broken twigs, upturned stones and strands of hair on brambles don't fade with time or weather."

"Smart little bitch!" He nipped her ear then licked it and pressed his body alongside, his joy at their reunion being beyond mere words.

He suddenly sat upright again. "It was *you* I saw in the shadow of the wall the night I got shot!"

"Who else?"

"But why have you never let me know you were there? Why let me suffer so, thinking I'd never see you again?" D'Arcy asked plaintively, and his eyes filled with pain.

"For just that reason. I would have weakened your resolve. Could you have let me return without you?"

"I suppose not. So it was you who left the birds and rat outside the den?"

"Until I knew you had met with the she-wolf and could be sure she would feed you. So tell me, how did you survive your wounds?"

"You're right, I was found by Moon-song – but you must have seen us together. Anyway, she led me to the hidden grotto, licked my wounds and cleared the infection with bark and herbs," D'Arcy began, then quickly related the bones of his story, but without disclosing the actual events of the night of the Solstice. However, judging from her expression and knowing look, Destiny did not need it spelling out. He began to realise that she knew more about the nature of the Quest than he had guessed.

Something else niggled at the back of D'Arcy's mind, causing him to frown and nibble his lip with frustration. Then the switch clicked and a blinding light flashed on: *Where is she? Has she gone and left you on your own, mate?* The words of the man now rang with a different significance. "He meant *you*, Destiny not Moonsong!" he exclaimed. "You got the man to feed you first, then led him to my hideout, knowing he would then leave food for me when you made the return journey home."

"Had to see you were fed, you being hopeless at hunting and all!" she said casually.

"You saved my life again Destiny!"

"Let's go, D'Arcy," she said gruffly, returning the pressure along his flank. "You can return now with honour. There is nothing more for you here."

"I'm still not sure about the purpose of it all."

"The Silver Pelt will carry, and breed into her lines, your genetic gentleness and generosity of spirit, D'Arcy. And this will carry on through the generations of wolves loosed into the wild. Their ability to survive, their essential wolf spirit, will remain intact but be tempered by, if not a love of man, at least a tolerance and respect for his territory. This, as Grey Pelt knows, is the only way the wolf can return to this land and in turn be tolerated itself."

"You are very wise, sis," he said humbly.

"Time to go home, bro."

D'Arcy looked around him at this place that had been his home and refuge when times were bad, and raised his head to Lady Moon who was once again approaching the full. But now there was a palpable absence of pain and restlessness, and the pelt along his spine failed to bristle and simply felt normal.

"The full moon is also the time of Completions," Destiny said shrewdly.

He nodded. "Yes. I'm ready now." He paused and looked at her with pain and something like fear in his eyes. "How will they take my homecoming Des?" he asked uncertainly, "Will the Pack accept me? Will the Alpha-Pair forgive my absence and welcome me home?"

It was Destiny's turn to nip his ear. "Silly boy. They will be overjoyed; you are the returning hero! Now let's be off!"

D'Arcy led the way out of the clearing and through the forest to the plain beyond.

It was as they emerged from the wood that they heard it, so faint as to be barely audible. Had they not both stopped and turned at that same moment, D'Arcy might have put it down to an over-excited imagination. They stood together, side by side, ears splayed to pick up the sound. It rose on the night like a wisp of wood smoke curling up from a smouldering fire and spiralling as it gathered height: a long, ululating, eerie and yet incredibly beautiful howl that was somehow feminine and, D'Arcy instinctively knew, meant for him alone. He also knew that she had sought him out with Moon-song's blessing. Somehow Moon-song had survived and reared the Silver Pelt, and today had brought her to him. As though she had picked up on his thoughts a second voice joined in, more resonant and mature yet reaching the same heights of heart-wrenching poignancy. *Moon-song.* He would know her song anywhere, and his heart filled with joy. He would not, could not, answer the howl for that part of him had now gone, or at least was buried deep again, but his heart went out to them both in a fond farewell. Moon-song and their lovely daughter would feel it on the wind. Separated by location, lifestyle and species, they nonetheless shared a common bond. His experience with the wolves had imbued him with intense pack loyalty and courage to defend its members from any danger. A part of him would stay within the Wolf Pack, and through the genes of the Silver Pelt, wolf ferocity would be tempered by compassion. Yet his heart ached for what could not be, and for what could never be told. He consoled himself with the memory of that first blue-eyed image of Moon-song in the clearing, one he would never forget. Now he recognised the preciousness of her gift. Who knew what perils she had risked, what taboos had been broken and what she might face upon her return to the Pack? She had made their daughter known to him, and nobody could take that away, or that moon-struck image of her in the forest.

As the last note wavered and faded Destiny looked deep into her brother's eyes and what he saw there was love, pride and understanding. She licked him on the nose and nudged him forward onto the track that snaked over the moor. As they moved forward together, a piercing cry and sudden rush of wind made them look up in time to see Hushwing Ghost-Owl sailing by. She swerved and glided directly above them, then with a jubilant screech dipped in greeting before rising again and disappearing into the night. So Hushwing had not deserted him either, D'Arcy thought with gratitude, knowing she would pick up on his thoughts, just as he had understood her flight of praise and congratulation. Destiny was right, he thought, loping by his sister's side in the moonlight. His task complete, he could return with honour to Alpha-He, the Pack, and his beloved Alpha-She. At last he was going home.

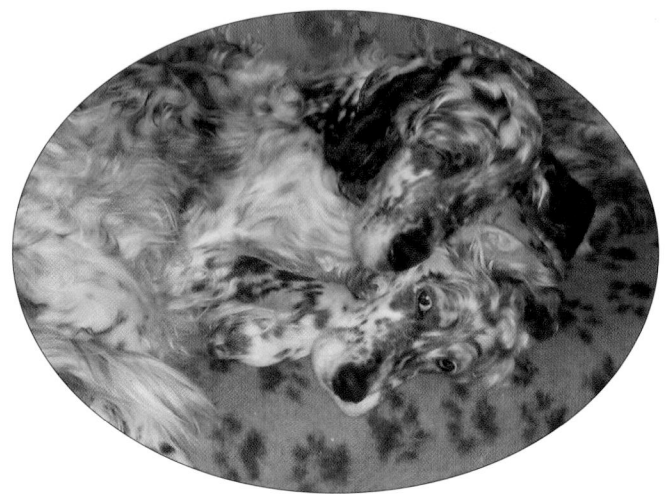

Brotherly Love: D'Arcy reunited with Destiny

19.

Homecoming

Spring arrived earlier in the valley than up on the fell and high moor and despite an early thaw and newness of the year, in the moonlight the first leaf buds were already to be seen on tree and hedgerow. As they trotted weary but elated along the sward, that wonderful end-of-winter and just-before-Spring earthy sweetness rose up from the ground beneath their pads as they travelled. They drew ever nearer to their own territory and D'Arcy's heart thumped inside his ribcage with excitement and apprehension. Destiny every now and then turned her head to give him a quick nod and a look of reassurance that said: 'It's okay, bro, trust me!' The fell and grassy foothill was left behind and their feet paced first the valley road, then the dusty, rutted surface of the narrow bridleway that wound its way to their home. Soon the End Fell Gate came into view and they were through it and on their own land at last. D'Arcy stood for a moment watching as the uppermost rim of the sun inched above the jagged ridge of the mountain pass in the east, and the silver grey of dawn shafted slowly across the surface of Merlins Mere. A mallard duck and her drake paddled haphazardly round to the other side of Birch Tree Island, the ripples in their wake highlighted and rimmed with pewter. The plish-plash of water and the cheerful trilling of a robin filled his heart with joy. The scene was spellbinding – and the beauty all the more precious for being 'home'. He would never, he vowed, ever leave it again.

"How do you want to do this, bro?" Destiny asked, standing alongside to look up inquiringly at him.

"We'll hang around here awhile, sis," he said nervously, looking around at their familiar and beloved pool, wood and foothills. "There's no need to disturb them, we can wait until everyone is awake."

"Okay. Whatever you say," Destiny said nodding. She stood quietly for a moment, then a slow grin spread over her elfin, upturned face.

"Don't be daft! Like hell there isn't – and to hell with waiting! Let's go make Alpha-She the happiest person alive! Race you home, slowcoach!" And with a wiggle of her butt and a cheeky grin she set off at high speed, her paws kicking up dust as they pounded the path that ran the length and breadth of the pool. After only a moment of hesitation, D'Arcy set off in pursuit, his now lean body and muscled legs striding the distance with ease. Even so, he surreptitiously slowed his pace as he caught up with Destiny, allowing her to be first to reach Lower Fell Gate.

Once in sight of the house he needed no directing or urging. Destiny stood back, content now to watch. He loped to the end of the house, threw back his head and barked beneath the window of Alpha-She's bedroom. That bark came from his belly and his heart and he kept on barking. He had expected the curtains to be flung apart and a puzzled face to appear at the window, but instead it was the door that was sent flying back against the wall with a bang, and Alpha-She rushed out in her nightclothes and on bare feet. She would know that bark anywhere, he realised as she suddenly halted, hand to heart, to stand and stare as though still afraid it might be a dream. He too stood immobile, and met the heartrending force of her gaze. His love for her streamed forth in palpable waves and shone too from his eyes, piercing the film of illusion.

"D'Arcy!"

He felt it was meant to be a cry, but it came out as a choked whisper. Tentatively he took a step towards her, then another and that was as far as he got; she rushed to meet him and dropped to her knees to enfold his emaciated body in her arms. "My boy. My beautiful boy! It really *is* you!" she whispered, squeezing him until he could scarcely breathe and he felt her tears of joy dripping onto his head. He leant against her and buried his head in her breast. Now he was truly home.

The reunion with the pack was no less emotional. Miss Tickle was the first to come, nosing her way round the door – left open by Alpha-She – to investigate the cause of the commotion that had so disturbed her slumbers. She saw D'Arcy, blinked twice, looked again then emitted a series of excited yelps and her tail thumped a tattoo against the timbers. Despite ample curves and advanced years she shot through the opening in a headlong rush, skidded to a halt before D'Arcy and licked every inch of his face. "My darling boy!" she panted in between licking, "oh, what a wonderful day! You are back with us again!"

A sleepy-eyed but excited Pippa was next, followed closely by Flossie and Fenella who tumbled forward with eyes alight, tongues lolling and tails waving wildly, but then the three girls slowed and advance sedately. After all, this was their Uncle D'Arcy and the Pack's new Top Dog. Not wishing to disappoint their expectations, D'Arcy stood for a moment in state, with head raised, chest puffed out and a stance worthy of any champion.

Then he blinked, pranced and dipped in the play-bow, inviting them all to share in his joy.

A few mad moments followed, with much barking and yipping and rushing about, and watched by Alpha-She amidst mingled tears and laughter, and a misty-eyed but satisfied-looking Destiny. The window was flung open and a tousled-headed Alpha-He demanded to know what the hell was going on, then paused open-mouthed as he took in the scene below. "D'Arcy!" he exclaimed, and the head abruptly disappeared. Alpha-He emerged from the doorway in his pyjamas and slapped D'Arcy on the back and fondled his ears. "Good man, D'Arcy," he said gruffly in the way that men greet one another, "Knew you'd be back lad," then forgetting all manly reserve he dropped onto his hunkers and hugged his boy whispering, "Welcome home, D'Arcy. So very, very glad to have you back!" and his eye glistened with something suspiciously like a tear.

Then, as though they had all only that moment realised that one of their number was missing, everyone stopped cavorting and stared at the doorway. Clifford stood in the opening, head up and chest out and looking every inch the Acting Top Dog. The pack members exchanged meaningful and even anxious glances. How would Clifford take D'Arcy's return and his own demotion from office? All eyes turned to Alpha-She for guidance. She stood relaxed and still and serenely smiling, telling them without words that she had confidence in her boys and that everything would turn out exactly as it should. D'Arcy blinked and moved forward a step, inviting Clifford to approach. Clifford moved forward, tail waving and stood before D'Arcy. Everyone held their breath for the next move.

"Boy, am I glad to see you back mate!" Clifford exclaimed, giving D'Arcy a friendly nudge with his muzzle, and everyone breathed normally again.

"Hey, not as glad as I am to be back!" D'Arcy gave Clifford's ear a playful nip. "Thanks for looking after things here, mate.

Destiny told me what a great job you've done. It can't have been easy!"

"Well, no it wasn't!" Clifford confessed, rolling his eyes to the sky and sticking out his left ear. "But Tickle was fantastic as always; couldn't have done it without her – and Destiny too, when she was here."

Ignoring for a moment the Alpha-Pair, D'Arcy addressed the Pack.

"I didn't expect such a wonderful welcome, and have no expectations after being away for so long. I had my reasons but cannot explain. I just want to say that it's enough to be accepted into the Pack, and that I'm more than happy for things to continue as they are," he finished, indicating Clifford with a turn of his head.

There was a moment of silence whilst the others looked uncertainly at one another.

"Well I'm certainly not!" Clifford said roundly, turning to stare at the other pack members. "Well, do you want D'Arcy as your Top Dog or not?"

Judging by the tumultuous response, the answer was an unequivocal 'Yes!'

D'Arcy swallowed hard and blinked rapidly several times, plainly overcome.

"Then with Clifford at my side, I shall do my best to honour both Joey and his Pack," he said at last, in a voice thick with emotion.

"Good, that's settled then!" Alpha-She said with a twinkle in her eye as she noted Alpha-He's puzzled expression. "Now, we'll get you fed, bathed and de-knotted. Lead *your* Pack indoors, Mr D'Arcy!" she added, nudging him forward.

"We make a good team, Destiny girl," Tickle was heard to whisper loudly as they trotted into the house. "You, me and Alpha-She are damned good fettlers and no mistake!"

With a wiggle and shimmy commendable in a girl half her age, Miss Tickle strutted through the door behind the new Pack Leader.

20.

An unsettling time for D'Arcy
. . . and Marley comes in
from the cold

D'Arcy was duly bathed, wrapped in a warm robe then dried and groomed until every last leaf, gorse sprig, knot and tangle were removed from his coat and he was sleek and handsome again, albeit much leaner than before. Alpha-She scarcely left his side and when forced to do so for one reason or another, hurried back again as though to make sure that he really was there and it was not just some wonderful dream. The Pack fussed and sniffed around him clamouring to know where he had been, whom he had seen and to hear the bones of his story. Nanny Tickle stepped in and declared that now was not the time and that D'Arcy could relate some of his adventures in a couple of day's time and after lights-out, the best time of all for telling a story.

"Mind, there will be things not meant for our ears, so no pressing him if he is unable to answer all our questions," she said firmly, with a wink for D'Arcy.

"Now let the lad have his space," she said watching D'Arcy shrewdly, "it will take a while for him to settle down to our boring ordinary life!"

At this the others melted away to do their own thing and D'Arcy threw her a grateful look.

In truth, settling back into normal life was proving harder than he could have imagined. After the loneliness and isolation of the fells, high moors and sweeping skies, he was finding the close proximity of so many others wonderful but also fatiguing and a tad stressful; their close and constant presence seemed to restrict his breathing and make him hot and bothered. Other things that he should have been glad of stressed him too, like the warmth of the Aga that now made him pant and his tongue loll and drip after the intense cold he had recently endured; that and the restricted space and expectations of how to behave and the routine of where and when. He felt like the most ungrateful wretch alive and was crushed by feelings of guilt. But he never felt stressed by the presence of Alpha-She. She allowed him space, and sensing his need, took him out with her for rambles around the pool and over the fell that she had roamed and come to know so well since the day he left them. Sensing his need to go off for a while and think, she would perch on a rock or fallen tree and patiently wait for him to return.

Towards the end of that first week he began to feel normality and routine stamping itself on his life and whilst he had not forgotten – and probably never would – that other life, the relinquishing of freedom and responsibility in return for love and security was ever easier to embrace. In moments of reflection, he had to admit to himself that he had never been truly independent; unable to hunt to survive, he had relied upon others to provide sustenance; first Hushwing, then Destiny (as he now knew) followed by Moon-song and finally the Man. The very thought of returning to that lonely, friendless and comfortless existence was enough to send him running in search of the Pack and Alpha-Pair. Gradually he not only grew used to the close proximity of the others but actively sought their constant companionship which he now saw as the most precious of gifts. English Setters are not meant to rough it alone on the mountains, he told himself with a lop-sided grin, they are meant for loving and spoiling and soft living and in return, he realised with sudden insight, we give our heart and soul.

However, what really brought him down to earth was a Pack Story-fest. This he had missed more than anything; it was the stuff of bonding and the epitome of what it meant to be a Setter-pack member. The passing on and keeping alive of the Pack Chronicles was where it was really at. Dinner had been eaten, chewies enjoyed and the pack members were lazing around the Aga winding down before supper and bed. Each day he had been aware of Destiny's eye upon him and now he saw her giving him a speculative look from beneath her white lashes. She worries I won't settle back into domestic life, he thought, pretending he had not noticed. She sat up, stretched and gave a huge yawn.

"Oh come on, someone, liven things up with a story!" she exclaimed, covering her mouth with a dainty paw as a second yawn threatened, giving the impression of boredom as opposed to deviousness.

"Yeah! Let's have a story!" Flossie cried, also sitting up sharply and looking keen. "Whose got one to tell?"

"I told mine," Fenella said looking disappointed.

"Never mind, Little One," Nanny Tickle said comfortingly, "You'll have plenty more to tell by the time you're my age!"

"What about Marley and the fatal fumes?"

"Oh yes! So who's going to tell it?" Flossie clamoured, looking hopeful.

"You know what," Destiny said with a sidelong glance at the door, "I think there may be someone just waiting for a chance to tell that tale for himself."

"Like who?" Clifford said frowning, then exclaimed as he followed her gaze, "Oh no! Not that damned—"

"Clifford!" Nanny Tickle warned, holding up a paw in admonition. "Don't be unkind now! After all, he did save—" then she looked swiftly at D'Arcy, then Destiny and put a paw over her mouth, "—anyway, I'm with Destiny on this one."

"Well nobody else seems to be offering," Pippa commented philosophically, "so I say 'why not?'!"

"You're out-voted, Cliffie!" Destiny said with a grin and a cheeky look.

"What's this all about? Did something happen whilst I was away?" D'Arcy said, looking from one to another.

"Let's invite Marley in to tell you," Destiny said, moving carefully to the doorway so as not to scare him away. "Marley, we'd like you to come and join us," she said turning her head to give Clifford a warning look, "and tell us your story."

Marley sat that very still and eyeballed Destiny while the clock on the wall above the door loudly ticked away the seconds.

"So are you coming in?" Destiny pushed the door wider.

"Suppose I might."

"You'll be quite safe."

"I know that," he said scornfully looking up at the ceiling, "But will you?"

Destiny grinned and retreated. "You're an Okay Cat, know that?"

Destiny perfectly understood Marley; they played the same tune and danced to nobody else's.

"Sit down, mate," Clifford said, in an effort to make amends for his earlier malice.

"Prefer to stand, thanks."

"Suit yourself," Clifford said sniffing, and he settled down by the Aga with his head turned away. The others, except for Destiny who was patently relaxed in his proximity, shifted from time to time and looked ill at ease. Eventually, however, Marley perched on the kitchen table and began his story, and everyone forgot to be nervous of tooth and claw as they listened.

"I didn't ask to come here, you know," he began in his usual crusty manner. "I was a pampered and highly-thought of cat, not one of your flea-bitten strays. My old mistress had fallen and been taken away in a big loud machine with flashing blue lights. It was the depths of winter – white everywhere and freezing, inside as well as out! Strangers came. They let the Aga go out and the fire too and turfed me outdoors and locked up the house. Me – who used to sleep under the covers with my mistress, her only companion, and now suddenly I was a nobody, out in the cold! Don't mind telling you, thought it was heap o' bones found under the tree for me!

"Well, nobody thought about me, did they? Except your Alpha-She who got the door open and brought food each day and cleaned my tray 'cos I couldn't get out to toilet or if I did, couldn't get back in again. Anyway, at least I was indoors. Bloody freezing in there mind, but a tad better than outside! But they had drawn the curtains and it so dark I ended up well confused – couldn't tell day from night. Worse thing though was the ghosts!"

"Ghosts? *Real* ones?" Mouths dropped open and eyes popped. Marley's ears went back and flattened against his head and eyes became huge and stared straight ahead in panic. He began to stammer and shake and visibly tremble as he continued:

"Yes, for real. They came out of the woodwork, yes, yes they did, and the old spice cupboard – there were nearly two thousand in there!" he gabbled.

171

"Hang on, how do you know that?" Clifford demanded.

"It had 1785 carved on the door – and that's near enough ain't it?" Marley snapped, momentarily recovering his air of bravado to air his knowledge. "My mistress was an educated lady and taught me all about numbers!"

"Seems an awful lot to me," Clifford grumbled, but made no further challenge and Marley scowled at him and continued:

"Anyway, they came through the cracks in the floor and the gaps round the windows – came whistling in with the wind!" Here he lost it again and began to quiver and quake. "White and wailing they were and glowing in the dark, and some just silent and wafting a stink like dead mice that I'd killed a few weeks back and left to rot. I got behind the settee, yes, poor Marley squashed up against the cold wall, no-one to help him, nobody there – only these stinking, vengeful ghosts. Night after flamin' night, day after day, they plagued me – not that I could tell the difference. They tweaked my whiskers when I was asleep and peed on my food and milk and whispered bad things in my ears. I was a pampered cat and reduced to this – I was living a nightmare and wished I was dead!

"So when your Alpha-She came with that cage I didn't waste time thinking about it. "It's so cold and spooky in here, and no place to spend Christmas Eve!" she said, looking round with a shiver. "Would you like to come and live with me?" She opened the door of the cage and I shot inside. She looked pleased as she closed it again, but puzzled too. "Guess that is a 'yes'! I thought we'd have a battle to get you inside," she added, "but it is horrible in here." And she shivered again and looked around her with the little light she kept in her pocket because the ones in the house didn't work anymore. "Let's get you out of here cat!" she said, "We'll need to give you a name. Reckon as it is Christmas and so spooky in here, we'll have to call you Marley!" Wasn't sure about the connection there, but figured she was an intelligent She-cat and must know what she was about. Anyway, couldn't have cared less if she'd called me 'Mousey', I just wanted outa there!

Well that was it, she brought me back here and you know the rest."

Marley arrives at Christmas

"Crikey mate, no wonder you're a tad . . . well . . ." Clifford exclaimed then stopped in mid-sentence, aware that he was about to put his paw in it yet again.

"Mad? Mad Marley you mean?" he snapped, but Marley sat up straight and his whiskers curled with something suspiciously like pride so they got the impression he wasn't averse to the tag. Clifford opened his mouth to protest then deemed it wiser to close it again and say nothing.

"Bolshi and defensive, he was going to say," Destiny soothed, "and none of us here can wonder at it, can we?" She turned to the others who shook their heads dolefully, tutted and muttered beneath their breath, and there were muted cries of 'shame' and 'shouldn't happen to anyone, mate'.

"Well now Marley, we want you to tell us now about the night you saved the Pack and the Alpha-Pair," Miss Tickle said in her best Pack Guardian and Elder voice.

"Okay, if you like. Your Alpha-pair had a new stove put in – to keep me warm at night, I guess," he said preening and pausing to raise one white paw, give it a leisurely lick and clean the tip of his nose. The others looked at each other and tried not to smile. "Well, you know I sleep in the sitting room, so why else would they have done it?" he said haughtily, noting their amusement.

"Dead right, Marley," D'Arcy said, giving the others a stern look, but winking at the same time. "You carry on with your story, little mate."

"Thank you. Anyway, Alpha-He stoked it up each night and closed it all down so it burned slow and kept me snug. Oh, it did that okay, except next morning I could hardly breathe! There was something wrong with that damn stove – but how to let them know? I tried telling them loudly but was just told to be quiet or I would disturb you lot! The next night I tried scratching at the door but got into lumber for that too. Next morning I felt worse than ever: my head hurt, my eyes were blurry and it was even harder to breathe.

"Okay, Marley, I told myself – this calls for drastic action. That night I tried all the same ways to warn them but again they took no notice. So as Alpha-He was shutting the door, I stalked over to the wood basket, jumped on top, wriggled my bum to make sure he knew what I was about, and did my pee on the wood!"

"You never!" Flossie exclaimed with a horrified expression.

"In front of Alpha-He?" You really are mad!" Clifford said, nodding vigorously as though justifying his earlier gaff.

"What did he do?" D'Arcy asked, curious.

"Picked me up, opened the window and chucked me out, just as I had planned!" Marley stated with obvious pride.

"Wow, that's brill!" Pippa exclaimed.

"Yep, I take it all back mate," Clifford said nodding again.

"And brave," Little Fenella piped up, "You could have got yourself thrown out for good."

"But surely he shut the window again? I remember the Big Freeze was around that time," Tickle said looking confused.

"He did that first time – once I was back inside. But I did it again the next night and he bawled for Alpha-She to get out of bed and sort 'this blasted cat!' She came blinking and rubbing her eyes and asking what the hell all the noise was about. Alpha-He angrily explained about me using the log basket for a loo and what was he supposed to do?

"Alpha-She was quiet for a moment and stood watching me thoughtfully. I tried my hardest to send her pictures first of the ghosts down the lane, then a sick cat sitting here by the stove. She frowned and looked confused for a time but I felt something was getting through. Eventually, she turned to Alpha-He and explained, "He had a bad time at his old place. He was left in the cold and dark for weeks at a time, and it was so, well, *spooky* in there. Sounds daft I know, but I think he was being 'got at'. I wouldn't stay there alone, I don't mind telling you!"

"So what has that to do with this?" Alpha-He demanded, running a hand through his hair in exasperation.

"It means we have to be patient with him."

"But we can't have the place stinking of pee!"

"I agree. So leave the window open, just a tad so he can get through. That's what he was used to before things went wrong at his old place."

"But it's minus nine outside!" Alpha-He protested.

"Freeze or stink – take your choice!" Alpha-She said crisply, turning to go back to bed. Just when I was thinking she had missed the point of the exercise, she stopped, frowned and came back into the room. "You know, the air doesn't feel quite right in here."

"How do you mean?" (Alpha-He had a head cold and had lost his sense of smell).

"It doesn't feel fresh or smell right – sort of 'cokey' and it makes me want to cough. We both have bad chests and head-aches that we haven't had before. Do you think he is trying to tell us something?"

"Like what?"

"Well, you spend a lot of time in here and you are worse than I am. I've heard you coughing real bad when I'm in bed."

"You think there's something wrong with the way the stove's been put in?"

Alpha-He looked and sounded alarmed.

Alpha-She shrugged then said simply "Just leave that window open," and went back to bed.

"Anyway, Alpha-He took it on board and bought a gadget that shows if the air is poisonous. That evening they got me out of the room and closed the window and door and left this thing inside. A short time after they went back inside and it must have told them something real bad because all hell broke lose! There was lots of shouting and they flung open all the windows, and the outside door and when they came out, shut the inside door too.

"We'll let the fire go out and it mustn't be relit! Nobody goes in there tonight!" Alpha-He ruled firmly. "We have to get checked out, like urgent!" he added, and sounded quite panicky to me!

"What about the Setters?" Alpha-She cried, and she was in even more of a panic.

"We'll test the kitchen and doggy den now," Alpha-He said, marching in that direction.

"So what happened?" D'Arcy broke in, his eyes wide with horror on hearing all this. The others already knew from snippets they had seen and heard, but they also looked aghast as it was the first time they had heard it from Marley's own mouth.

"The kitchen and den checked out okay, so no more panic about you lot! The Alpha-Pair went to hospital and were tested and given medicine for their poorly chests. I heard them laughing about the doctor saying 'that cat of yours gave up a couple of his nine lives for you two, because the open window has saved you', but they must have believed it because I got an extra saucer of cream a day! Anyway, that's the end of my story," he finished abruptly.

There was a moment or two of silence as the Pack took in the enormity of what they had heard. Marley's laid back style did nothing to detract from the horror of the potential disaster, or the value of what he had done.

"Thank you for telling us your tale, and for saving all our lives too!" Nanny Tickle said graciously at last.

"It was nothing." Marley coughed and looked embarrassed but also pleased – and puffed up to twice his normal size.

"Marley, you are a hero!" Destiny stated simply.

"Great stuff little fella," Clifford said, and the others all joined in the praise.

"Tell you what, you come and join our story-fests whenever you please," Clifford added generously.

"Yes, do!" the others chorused.

"You'll be more than welcome!" D'Arcy said solemnly, rising to stand before Marley who was perched on the table still. "On behalf of the Pack, I can never thank you enough. If it hadn't been for your quick thinking, I might have returned to a terrible tragedy."

"Very true, but we won't go there!" Nanny Tickle intervened, picking up on D'Arcy's air of despondency and guilt. "it could just as easily have happened when you were here, and there would have been nothing you could have done D'Arcy," she added wisely, and D'Arcy nodded and looked brighter.

"Right, good night all – I'm off to my bed," Marley said brusquely, jumping down from the table to stalk to the door.

"Just one thing," D'Arcy said, stopping him in his tracks.

"What's that then?" Marley said looking suspicious.

"You keep talking about 'your' Alpha-Pair."

"So?"

"They are now *your* Alpha-Pair too!" D'Arcy said, and turning to face the others he added, "I vote Marley an honorary member. What do you say, Pack?"

"Sure thing!" they chorused.

"Okay, no problem with that," Marley said coolly, but as he stalked from the kitchen he carried his head up high and his tail rose vertically in the air. He also walked with a noticeable swagger.

Marley at his new home come Spring

Clifford   D'Arcy

21.

Momentous news and D'Arcy reaches an understanding with Clifford – and Alpha-She

About a week later Alpha-She brought to Alpha-He's attention an item of remarkable news, and the Pack lay about the kitchen and listened with great interest. "Have you seen this?" she exclaimed, brandishing the local newspaper.

"Haven't read the paper yet – why, what is it?"

"You remember me telling you about that pilot wolf project set up by the University and Defra? Yes, yes, you do, it was over at Weirdale," she said impatiently as Alpha-He shook his head. "At the time it caused a lot of controversy, especially within the farming community. They released several wolves into restricted territory."

"Oh yes, I do now." Alpha-He put down the gardening book he had been browsing and gave his full attention. "They closed the valley off from public access. So what has happened, a breakout?"

"Not that! You remember the original wolves split off into two packs? Well a third pack of just a couple of wolves has been sited."

"Yeah, that's interesting." But Alpha-He was frowning as wondering why she should be looking so flushed and even anxious. He was also puzzled by D'Arcy's sudden alertness and air of intensity.

"And guess what?"

"I've no idea, but I bet you're about to tell me!" Alpha-He said mildly.

"Dead right I am! One of them is a hybrid!"

"Ah, I see. So a farm dog over that way has been making hay!" Alpha-He said with a grin. "Or should I say sowing oats!"

D'Arcy drew in a sharp breath and on hearing it, Alpha-She turned and gave him a strange look then turned back to Alpha-He. "Who says the dog was male?" she challenged, "It could have been a male wolf who took a collie bitch or whatever."

"True. But I don't mind guessing the other member of the new pack is a she-wolf! Otherwise the offspring wouldn't be accepted."

"Maybe. It doesn't say here," Alpha-She said casually, folding the newspaper as though to close the subject.

All that day D'Arcy was aware of the Pack members' eyes upon him. "So what was that all about?" Clifford asked as they followed the Alpha-Pair to the fell for the daily run and game of 'catch the treat'.

"All what?" D'Arcy parried.

"You know, back there," Pippa said boldly, matching her stride to the boys.

"Why did Alpha-She keep giving you strange looks?" Flossie pressed, joining the others.

"Don't know what you're on about!" D'Arcy snapped, and trotted off up the fell and out of their reach.

"Leave off, you lot!" Destiny ordered and the younger girls fell back. "Be patient, and maybe you'll learn something tonight!"

The youngsters clamoured to know more, but Destiny followed D'Arcy and ignored their entreaties.

That evening after dinner the questions began again.

"What happened when you were away D'Arcy?"

"Why did you stay away so long when you knew Joey had left us?"

"What was so important, more important than us?"

Gradually the questions became more aggrieved in tone as the Pack released pent-up feelings of loss and resentment suppressed in the excitement and relief of D'Arcy coming home. As the tension rose and D'Arcy looked more and more uncomfortable, Destiny stepped in. "Shhhh! I feel a song coming in!"

She sat very upright and still, ears back and open, eyes glazed and far-seeing. Obediently the Pack fell silent and waited. Destiny's songs from beyond were to be treated with respect. She remained like that for several minutes then began to sing in a high keening voice:

Silver Pelt's Song

There's a legend in the Wild-packs
Handed down from long ago,
Of a strange blue-eyed creation
With a pelt of dappled snow.

It tells of Grey Pelt's vision
And the hope of his ghostly pack,
That the Silver Pelt will calm Man's rage
And bring the wild wolves back.

181

Half flesh and half immortal
She is born of one of each,
And her song will rise on midnight wings
Along with Hushwing's screech.

But is any soul brave enough
Amongst those who carry His sign,
Of a moon-struck ridge of darkened pelt
That strengthens nerve and spine?

She will be the shining outcome
Should one dare to plight his troth,
Born of loyalty and courage
She will bear the best of both.

As she pads across the forest floor
Moon-dappled and aflame,
Have faith and recognise her birth
By calling out her name.

She stands for tolerance and harmony,
And her lessons Man will learn,
For when the Silver Pelt appears on Earth
The Wild Wolves will return.

There were no more questions that night or any other. As the last haunting note died away the Pack members sat for a moment in silence and all eyes turned to D'Arcy. He sat upright and very still, chest out and head held high. Now the Pack knew the truth-that-could-never-be-spoken and the reason for his long absence. Now they were really *his* pack, and he could lead them with honour. One by one they filed past him and dipped their head in respect as they made their way to the beds.

"Thanks, sis," he whispered as they stood proudly side by side.

"They kept faith with you D'Arcy, and wanted you as leader without being aware of the reason behind your absence; they deserve to know."

"I'm lucky to have such a pack, and a sister like you, Destiny."

"Don't go all soppy on me – off you go to bed, bro!" she quipped, giving his ear a playful nip.

Later, as the pack lay sleeping on their beds by the Aga, feet twitching as they chased or were chased by the wild wolves in their sleep, Alpha-She crept to D'Arcy's side. She crouched by his bed for a moment caressing his head, one of his big paws tucked securely into her hand. Sensing her need, he pretended to be asleep, to be unaware of her presence to give her the confidence to speak.

"I understand why it had to happen D'Arcy, and you haven't betrayed me. I am so proud of you, and I think Grey Pelt must be too. Don't worry; your secret is safe with me. Maybe one day we shall see her."

So saying she kissed the top of his head then rose and walked to the door. He opened his eyes, looked straight at her and blinked twice, then rolled onto his back, feet in air, to let her know he had heard and was overjoyed.

By the glow from the nightlight he saw her nod and smile.

A day or so later as they ambled around the field nibbling on new growth and sniffing the fragrance of earth warmed by early Spring sunlight, Clifford drew alongside. "Good to feel Spring's on the way, isn't it?" he said conversationally, but throwing a nervous, sidelong glance at D'Arcy who was chewing on a fresh blade of grass. Before D'Arcy could answer Clifford rushed on: "That new song of Destiny's was really something, wasn't it? Sort of put us in the picture without telling, if you get what I mean. She's one helluva girl!"

"Best sis a guy could have," D'Arcy agreed, privately wondering where Clifford was going.

"Er, I've got something to tell you too, mate," Clifford stammered, his left ear sticking out as it always did when he was worried.

"Oh yeah? What's that?" D'Arcy's mind raced as he stood still and waited.

"Whilst you were away, well somebody asked for me, I mean you know Alpha-She has always wanted . . ."

"Spit it out, Clifford!" D'Arcy said sharply, his heart thumping.

"They brought a little girl to me from a place called Wales," Clifford confessed in a rush, "and now she's got my puppies!"

D'Arcy stared and remained silent whilst Clifford, wide-eyed and nervous, chewed his lip.

"Barking hell! I thought you were going to tell me you were leaving!" D'Arcy exclaimed at last.

"You mean you don't mind?" Clifford gasped, his ear slowly lowering along with his anxiety.

"I'd mind you leaving! You're my best mate! But no, of course not, why should I mind? Anyway, what's her name and how many?"

"She's called Blodwen and she's lovely, D'Arcy," Clifford said shuffling his feet and looking a tad embarrassed.

"You've fallen for her!"

"Guess so."

"Don't be embarrassed, I understand."

"Yes. Yes, I know you do." Clifford looked sympathetic. "Anyway, we have nine lovely puppies."

"*Nine,* you say! Wow, Clifford – you're a dark horse ain't you! Congratulations mate and well done!"

"Thanks, D'Arcy. Yes, six boys and three girls and I heard Alpha-She say they all look like me!" Clifford added proudly. "They're all doing fine; Blodwen is a super little mum."

"Good on her too then!"

Clifford walked on a pace or two, then turned to D'Arcy and worry clouded his lustrous eyes. "There's something else . . ." he started to say.

"When is he coming?" D'Arcy interrupted.

Clifford's mouth dropped open. "You know?"

"I know that Alpha-She has always wanted a little blue boy – a Benson. Your little boys are Ben's great grandsons – can you see it? One of your boys not coming here? Of course not! It's unthinkable!"

"That's big of you D'Arcy."

"No, it's big of you Clifford to have made Alpha-She so happy. Anything that does that is okay by me! Especially as I made her so sad. I wish I could have spared her that; the pain of thinking I might never return and even be dead."

"She never stopped looking for you D'Arcy. And she always believed you were alive and would one day return. She told us that constantly, when we were missing you and feeling down. You are very special to her."

D'Arcy sighed and shook his head. "It has been a hard time for us all; I cannot help but feel responsible."

"You didn't exactly have an easy time of it either from what I can gather, being shot and all! Besides, Destiny had it right with her song; something wonderful has happened because of your courage and faithfulness to the Quest!"

"You're a good lad, Clifford," D'Arcy said, affectionately flipping Clifford's ear with his nose. "Anyway, any addition to my Pack makes me bigger too!"

"Thanks again, mate." Clifford heaved a big sigh and visibly relaxed. "Been so worried, you've no idea. Couldn't believe you would welcome him".

"I can't do it myself, Clifford," D'Arcy said somberly. "As Alpha-She sometimes quotes: 'whereof one cannot speak, thereof one must be silent'.* You heard the song and know the score. But

---

* Ludwig Wittgenstein.

I can help *you* do it, if you'll let me. I'd like to share in bringing up the youngster, if that's okay with you?"

"I'll be honoured, D'Arcy. So will Benson."

"Good, that's settled then."

"I'm sorry you can't, well you know . . ." Clifford said haltingly.

"But I've seen her Clifford. I've *seen her*!"

They walked on in companionable silence; there was nothing more to be said.

Ben: And here they are, all nine of them with their lovely dam!

Eight good little puppies!

Blodwen . . .

. . . and Number Nine who
wouldn't lie still!

One of these six mischievous boys was destined to be named 'Benson' for me, heaven help him, and has now joined my earthly Pack. But Alpha-She sprang yet another surprise: she was unable to leave behind his twin sister Bronwen. Both have a neat black streak at the corner of the left eye – but as my father also had it, I trust he is responsible rather than Grey Pelt! And yes, of course I am proud. I'm proud of both my boys: D'Arcy for his open-hearted leadership and courage in following untrodden paths, and Clifford for giving Alpha-She her longed-for Baby Benson. It was always meant to be, but timing is all.

And here they are: my Great Grandson and Granddaughter:

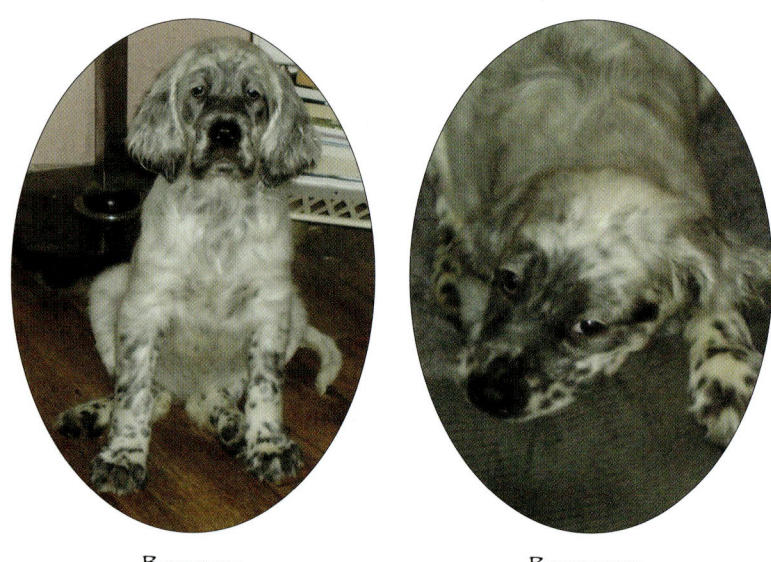

Benson   Bronwen

(Just arrived and 8 weeks old to the day)

The twins sharing a joke!

My son Joey has come home to me, and we pledge to look after the youngsters and guide them in the Way of the Pack. The part of me that is in Benson will rejoice at being with Alpha-She once more, and in seeing her face light up with gladness.

I'm so pleased you could join us again. I hope before long you will be saying 'hello' to Benson and Bronwen; no doubt at some stage you will be learning about their adventures too!

Thank you for sharing our tears and laughter; remember, it takes raindrops as well as sunlight to make a rainbow!

Ben 🐾

Rainbow on Merlins Mere

If you have enjoyed this book about
English Setters, and would like to know
more about the breed, why not try the
English Setter Association's book:

ENGLISH SETTERS INTO THE MILLENNIUM

Published by the
English Setter Association

There are contributions from experienced
ESA members specialising in diet, training,
health, grooming and breeding, etc.
The book is beautifully illustrated with line
drawings and colour photographs, and is
available direct from the ESA.

Details from the web site:
www.englishsetterassociation.co.uk

ALSO AVAILABLE . . .

Memories of a Moon Map
The Extraordinary Adventures of an English Setter Pack

NINA GREEN

From Amazon, or can be ordered at bookshops
or online direct from www.pendragon-press-ltd.co.uk

Also available in Pendragon by Nina Green . . .

DARK STAR

A novel of dark and chilling prophecy: the dark star of the North brings Retribution, Silence and Death. Estranged from her husband, reporter Darcy West reluctantly takes on her orphaned nephew Alisdair, who finds a strange meteor on a lonely Lakeland mountain. It falls into the hands of an unscrupulous physicist with terrifying consequences. Darcy battles greed and corruption, aided by Mr Ambrose, an elderly hermit with strange powers.

ISBN 0-9530538-0-6   £6.99 + pp

A GRAVE AFFAIR

Brutal murder and deadly passion: medieval lovers reach across the centuries in search of justice and revenge. Following a broken love affair, writer Jo Cavanagh sets off for a remote cottage in the heart of Lakeland to immerse herself in writing her latest book. Unknown to Jo a new grave is being dug at the tiny local church. *But is it new?* The terror begins as long-buried passions are released.

ISBN 0-9530538-1-4   £6.99 + pp

IMMORTAL DUST

The remains of a medieval knight are unearthed on the wild Cumbrian coast after being buried for 700 years: bizarre burial rituals have kept the body preserved. The find brings murder and betrayal in its wake. The second Darcy West book. Darcy is obsessed with the quest for this man's identity. Astronomy and alchemy, ritual and mysticism lead her into a maze where past and present intertwine. With Brant Kennedy she finds tempestuous love, but betrayal lurks in the shadows. A mystical union develops between Darcy, reporter in search of the ultimate story, and Anton, the knight with such a story to tell.

ISBN 0-9530538-2-2   £7.99 + pp

All are available on Amazon, or can be ordered at bookshops or online direct from www.pendragon-press-ltd.co.uk